Explicit Romance Novels (2 Books in 1)

True Erotic Sex Stories:

EXPLICIT DIRTY HOT NOVELS FOR WOMAN

Seductive Erotica

The most sensual and intriguing stories that you can also practice with your partner or your lover! Explode your sexuality with this book

This is a work of fiction. Names, character, places and incidents are either the product of the author's imagination or are used fictitiously, and any resemblance to actual persons, living or dead, business establishments, events or locales is entirely coincidental.

@ COPYRIGHT BY Jessica Dominate

All right reserved. No part of this book may be reproduced or used in any manner without written permission of the copyright owner except for the use of quotation in a book review.

Enough Gangbangs (Gangbangs)

Rachel remembers her gangbangs.

Rachel couldn't believe her eyes, the ad in the newspaper's Personal Section read:

Escorts needed for a writer's workshop.

Dates 3-1-13 to 3-15-13. Transportation,

room, board provided. Pay package includes

$10,000 plus tips. If interested contact

herb@XXX.XX

Making contact with Herb was an easy decision. She sent three nude pictures and one line of text: Too many parties, too many bars, too many drinks, not enough men.

She received a reply two days later.

You've been selected to participate in the writer's conference.

Contact Herb Brantley for more details.

She received a round trip ticket to Phoenix, Arizona and a check for one thousand dollars with instructions to meet Herb Brantley when she arrived.

* * *

Rachel was met at the airport dressed in a conservative dark-green business suit. A handsome man wearing a brown business suit stood beside a sign with her name on it.

"You're more beautiful than your pictures Ms. Grayson," he said offering her his hand.

She smiled shaking his hand. "Thank you."

"It's my pleasure; did you have a good trip?"

"Yes, but I'm looking forward to better ones while I'm here." She smiled naughtily brushing long red hair over her shoulders.

"We were impressed with your pictures but even more with your note: 'Too many parties, too many bars, too many drinks, but not enough men.'"

"I like my little aphorism."

"Does it have a meaning deeper than the obvious?"

"Do you think it's profound?"

"It's poetic in style and poems are usually multi-layered."

"The four stanzas are self explanatory and it's a short-hand way of describing my inclinations and personality, but I only wrote it to attract attention and get this gig."

"It worked." He offered her his arm and walked toward the terminal's entrance. "The conference is being attended by some of the best young writers in the country. We want them to leave pleased with the workshop, we want to sign as many of them as possible to book contracts with Coito Publishing, and you and the other escorts are to make the week as pleasant for them as possible." He smiled.

"In other words, you want us to fuck them as part of a package they can't refuse."

"I wouldn't have used those words but you have the general idea."

He led her toward the terminal's entrance.

She squeezed his arm. "How many will there be?"

He looked at her. "Twenty have accepted the invitation."

"A nice round number," she commented.

"There'll be a total of five escorts including you."

She grinned. "Twenty divisible by five how sweet."

"Are you being sarcastic?" Ms. Grayson.

"A little but I like large numbers and proportions. Do you fit either of those categories?"

He smiled at her. "I've never had a complaint."

"That's nice to hear." She rubbed her hip against his.

They stepped to the curb waiting for a white limo. A large black man dressed in a chauffeur's uniform helped Rachel and Herb into the vehicle.

"It's about a two hour drive to the Coito Ranch where the workshop will be conducted. Would you care for a drink?"

"A sweet white wine would be nice." She observed his fine ass as he bent to retrieve the wine from a small refrigerator.

He poured each of them half a flute.

She removed her jacket, unbuttoned the blouse, and pulled it open.

Herb handed her the wine and ogled her breasts covered by a white bra.

"Would you like a sample?" She poured wine on the tip of her bra revealing a rigid nipple. "I haven't been laid in days."

"We can't allow any wine to go to waste." Herb moved to suck her wet bra and nipple.

Before he got there she doused her other teat. Oh, that's cool."

On his knees, Herb licked the excess fluid from each nipple, and reached behind her to unfasten the hooks of her bra.

She assisted by raising her arms over her head.

He pulled the cups from under her plump tits and they vibrated falling to their natural position looking like pendulous melons.

He cupped them with his hands and kissed her ruby red lips.

She responded with a "Humm," and an accepting mouth and darting tongue.

The held each other for a long time with tongues entwining, has hand fondling her breasts, and her hands exploring his back side.

Rachel reacted to her teats being stimulated by pulling her green trousers from her waist and under her ass. "Suck," she commanded and went about the task of removing his tie and unbuttoning his shirt before unbuckling his belt and downing his zipper.

As the limo went around a curve they separated.

She scrambled to remove her panties and fished for his cock. "Oh, you've got a nice one, let me try it out." She straddled his lap, pulled her pussy lips apart, and spindled herself on his shaft groaning, "Aaaaugh, I needed that." She sat still enjoying being filled, and she lifted her breasts to his face. "Suck on both of them while I hump your staff."

He smiled and took one nipple into his mouth and fondled the other.

Resting on her haunches she slid up and down his erection. She felt his cock hardening and swelling. "Herb, you're not going to last long." Placing her hands on his shoulders, she drove her cunt as hard and fast as she could on him.

His breathing became faster, he perspired, he groaned, "Damn, damn, I'm coming already," and he lifted his hips to push deeper into her cavity as he lost control and ejected spurt after spurt into her.

She continued humping him until he became limp and slipped from her."

"Wow you're a great piece-of-ass." He pulled her close with his face buried between her breasts.

They were quiet for a while enjoying the release of sexual tension.

"Do we have enough time for seconds?" She asked crawling off of him.

He smiled. "Yes, but it'll take me a while to recover."

"Let's finish our wine. Do you have any food? Fucking always makes me hungry."

"Yes, I have some snacks." He pulled them from the refrigerator and poured them more wine. "You're going to be an incredible asset to this weekend. If you treat all men like you've treated me you may not get much sleep."

"I can go a week without sleep if I'm busy doing something else."

They ate, drank and talked.

She removed the rest of his clothes, and fondled his limp cock until it started to stiffen. "Aha, now we can have some more action." She got on the floor, rested her head on the seat, and spread her legs. "Give it to me doggie style, but I want you to play with my tits."

He shoved himself into her pussy, leaned over her back and grabbed her boobs. Holding on to her, he slowly thrust in and out, in and out. At the same time he hardened her nipples adding to his pleasure.

She was not close to an orgasm but she began to moan at each of his down strokes, "Oh, aah, yas, oof."

He rooted with increasing enthusiasm and quickened his speed and power.

"Use your finger on my clit."

He released one tit and placed the other on her honey button.

Circling his finger around her clit aroused Rachel. "Harder and faster," she cried.

Herb increased the speed of his stroking and the speed of his finger circling her clit.

"Oooah, nice, very nice, keep it up." She wiggled from side to side to increase her pleasure.

He was motivated to bring her to an orgasm, and he rammed her harder and faster as well as continuing to massage her clit.

"I'm getting close keep it up."

Going into overdrive, Herb pounded her faster and faster.

"Oh, oh," she said arching her back and clamping her pussy muscles hard around his staff until she exploded under him by moving in all directions and howling, "I'm coming, I'm coming, aaaaugh, ooooah, yooough, yes, yes, yes!"

He continued to hump her until he groaned, "Ah, ah, ah, God damn, God damn, that's one sweet pussy."

They slumped to the floor enjoying their orgasms. By the time they reached the ranch, they'd cleaned up using wipettes, and redressed.

She was delivered to a villa separated from the main lodge. Herb carried her luggage into the building and kissed her before left.

"Thank you Herb for one of the most enjoyable rides I've had in a long time. What's on the schedule for this evening?" She fondled his crouch.

There's going to be a cocktail party at seven, but be ready by 6:45 and dress to impress."

* * *

Rachel selected a black cocktail dress with abundant cleavage and lots of leg. At five feet eleven inches in height, four inch heels, a Lindsey Lohan look, long red hair, and a Playboy figure she expected to command interest.

She and the four other escorts were picked up by a large white van at 6:45 and taken to the Coito Ranch. It was a large building built of manufactured logs with a wrap-around porch. It had been designed to fit into the hilly, arid, and barren landscape. Its construction was the same style as the villa where she was housed.

Herb Brantley met them on the porch, passed out name tags and said "Mingle. Remember, we want them to have a really good time." He opened the door into a large room wonderfully designed and furnished in white pine panels and western style furniture. There were ten tables and chairs and two wet bars with four male bar tenders. The writers and Coito acquisitions staff were standing, sitting, conversing and drinking as the escorts entered.

Rachel was the last into the room. Her height plus four inch heels, flaming red hair, and voluptuous shape instantly attracted interest. She accepted white wine and stood talking with her admirers while surveying the room seeking the best looking or most interesting man to fuck. Everyone dressed casually, but one man sitting by himself attracted her. He was gorgeous wearing chinos and a blue shirt unbuttoned half way down his chest showing off the hair on his chest. He definitely had a non-conforming persona.

She excused herself from the mob and walked to him. "I'm Rachel Grayson and wonder why you're sitting by yourself." She extended her hand.

Standing, he shook her hand but didn't let go as he ogled her. "I'm Jet Ralston. Are you as beautiful under that dress as you are in it?"

"I think better. Would you like to find out?" She moved closer to him.

"I would but I must warn you I like kinky sex," he said seriously.

Her eyes opened wide. "What's your definition of kinky?"

"Blind folds, restraints, dildos, and cock rings for starters," he stared at her breasts, "and for you I believe nipple clamps would be appropriate."

She smiled. "Nice, do you follow BMSD rules?"

"Of course, the idea is to enjoy sex not to inflict pain. I'm into pleasure and it appears you have the same interests."

"I'm ready when you are." She nodded, smiled, and looked into his jet black eyes.

* * *

In his bedroom, he took her in his arms. "Has anyone told you today how beautiful you are?" Before she could answer, he kissed her and thrust his tongue into her mouth. One hand unzipped her dress, unfastened her bra, and he had her step out of her dress and panties. "I'm going to blindfold and tie you to the bed."

"You don't have to do that. I like to be active while being fucked."

"I understand but I'm doing it to increase our pleasure." He pushed her to the bed and bound her hands and feet to the four corners of the bed before climbing on to the bed above her head. With his hand on his shaft, he probed her mouth until she took it into her mouth. He fucked her face and leaned forward to fondle one breast and to suck the other nipple into his mouth. He sucked long and hard on both nipples as he continued humping her mouth.

Rachel liked to suck cock. His length and girth satisfied her oral instincts and his hand and mouth on her boobs stimulated her desire.

He pulled from her mouth. "Did you like that as much as I did?"

"Give it to me I'm ready," she whimpered and lifted her head to follow the sound of his movements to the side of the bed.

"If you liked that wait until you feel this." He placed lightly vibrating clamps on her nipples.

She moaned at the pressure and fluctuations the clips had on her teats. The feeling was different than his hands and mouth. "It hurts a little, but it's causing a hum in me."

"You won't notice any pain in a minute." He turned on a vibrating dildo and slowly circled the bed rubbing the throbbing instrument over her body.

Rachel relished the pulsating massage. She especially liked it as it ran up and down her inner thighs. "That tickles."

"It's supposed too." He turned the vibrator off and rubbed it around her pussy.

She giggled. "That's nice."

Her body tensed when the vibrator was turned on and used to massage her nipples and coursed over and around her cunt.

Over and over again he circled her twat while slowly increasing the speed of the dildo.

She writhed in pleasure.

He used one hand to pull the hood from her clit. He touched the honey button with the dildo.

The intensity of the vibrations was overwhelming and caused her pussy to contract and pushes her over the peak of passion into the throes of a major orgasm lasting almost a minute. She howled, "Oh God, oh God, oh God, I'm coming, I'm coming, aaaaaw!"

Before she recovered, his dick slammed into her. He pounded relentlessly, and she noticed a hard rubbery object strike her pubis bone and clitty as he stroked her.

When he tired she asked, "What are you wearing?"

He laughed long and loud. "I thought you might like some additional titillation so I put on a vibrating cock ring."

"I haven't felt any vibrations."

"I haven't turned it on yet, are you ready?"

"Is it going to be as stimulating as the dildo?"

"I don't know. Tell me what you think." He held the cock ring against her clit. He turned on the vibrator.

"Oh that's nice."

He pressed into her with all his weight and turned the vibrator on high.

She rose on her shoulders and feet bowing her back at the awesome sensations the cock ring vibrators gave her. The feeling was like the fire and heat of a lighting strike. She screamed, "Yaaaahgh, oooooah, whooo!"

As her contractions persisted, he stroked her with the zeal of a man gone crazy. He leaned to one side and then the other as he thrust in and out of her. His hips twirled in circles as he pounded her pussy. "Are you ready? I'm about to come."

"Give me your best shot." She rose on her shoulders and lifted her hips to give him a better angle. She felt the speed of his thrusting increase, his cock became more rigid, it expanded, and he shot his jism into her ready and eager pussy.

* * *

"I have a proposition for you," Herb said as he sat in Rachel's villa Monday after lunch.

"I like to be propositioned." She crossed her legs at the ankle.

He leaned forward with hands on his knees. "I've been overwhelmed by requests for your company."

"That's a wonderful complement. All of them want to spend quality time with me?" She asked eagerly.

"Yes and with your permission, I'll schedule you with four men every night this week."

"Four, is that all?" She laughed uncrossing her legs.

"You're in great demand, but you can't deal with that many at one time, so I've spaced them depending on their schedules. I'll arrange for you to be with them anyway you like: one on one, two threesomes, or a gangbang."

She stared into his brown eyes with her mouth open. "I've never been in a gangbang, so let's go for that. Five gangbangs in five nights. I'm so excited I'm wetting my panties."

He scowled. "Damn, I'd like to help you with your problem, but I have to work on the schedule and see to other details."

* * *

Rachel sat on a brown leather couch wearing a green gown and wondering how this gangbang would differ from the other four. The first night was exciting because none of them had ever been in a gangbang. The next three nights were variations of the first. She sucked and fucked a lot of dicks, but she didn't orgasm often due to the inexperience of her partners. She thought this night would be better because of the presence of Jet Ralston.

There was a knock on the door at eight o'clock and four casually dressed men carrying small bags filed into the room with Jet at the back.

She stood and asked," How would you gentlemen like to proceed?" Wiggling her shoulders, she allowed the gown to slip to the floor. They gawked at her pendulous breasts hanging like ripe fruit and the red thatch of hair covering the prize they sought.

Jet threw up his hands. "Okay guys, she's build like a brick shit house. You already knew that let's not forget the plan."

They quickly undressed and each of them took a limb and carried her into the bedroom. They laid her on the bed and from their bags they placed soft cloth cuffs around her wrists and ankles, and then to the four corners of the bed.

She lay restrained in a venerable spread eagle position, with her hips placed on a pillow, but was mentally prepared and excited about what was going to happen.

"I'm going to cover your eyes to intensify your feelings so we all have a good time," Jet said as he pulled a blindfold over her eyes.

She felt them crawling onto the bed; one near her head, one on each side, and one close to her feet. Nothing was said but almost simultaneously she was kissed passionately, two mouths took nipples into their mouths, and a hand roamed through her pubic hair and around her cunt and anus. The stimulations on all of her erogenous zones were arousing. Her tongue was entwined with another, her nipples were licked and sucked, and she was tickled around her most sensitive sex organ.

She felt and heard them moving around until someone was at each of the previous positions. A dick probed at her lips and she eagerly took it into her mouth. Vibrators were used to massage her chest, sides, stomach, and breasts. Another stimulator coursed through her pubic hair and around her twat, and a finger lubricated her asshole.

"I like what you guys are doing but I'm not comfortable with the ass play."

Another cock slipped into her mouth and she sucked enthusiastically. Vibrating clamps were placed on her nipples delighting her. At the same time other vibrators wandered over the remainder of her upper body. A dildo was slipped into her tunnel while at the same time a thin and short butt plug was placed in her anus.

"I told you before I don't like the butt plug." Aside from the invasion of her ass she enjoyed the good tasting cock in her mouth, the throbbing on her nipples and massaging of her body, and she especially liked the rod being run in and out of her passageway. She felt the signs of an impending orgasm.

They changed locations a third time. She sucked on the larger of the two cocks. The vibrations on her body and nipples increased in intensity, and the dildo was removed from her cunt. The butt plug was replaced with a larger one and the vibrator turned on high and placed on her clit. The gathering storm within her reached its peak from all the stimulations, and she spilled over into an orgasm, "Yaaaaugh, aaaaaah, ooooooah!

She was left alone for a minute. They climbed back onto the bed and a larger butt plug replaced the smaller one and the pillow was removed. Before she could complain a cock plunged into her, stopped deep within her, withdrew and rammed into her hard ten times. Not only did the cock affect her but each forward stroke caused the butt plug to bang into her. She was surprised by the suddenness of the two invasions and she grunted, "Aah," at each stroke. At the same she was kissed and her nipples licked and sucked.

The dick pulled out without coming, and another cock thrust into her and ceased for a moment and then gave her ten rough strokes. A larger butt plug pushed into her ass. She didn't have time to catch her breath before the staff thrust into her and she continued to grunt, "Aah, aah."

A third and then a fourth cock entered her roughly and gave her ten powerful strokes. Each cock and each stroke added to her pleasure and when the fourth man massaged her clit as he pounded her sent waves of electric-like shocks throughout her body and mind and she climaxed with a howl: "I'm coming, I'm coming, I'm coming, daaaaaamn!"

Her bounds were released from the bed but not her wrists and ankles. She was lifted, the butt plug removed, and her anus was lowered to the tip of a hard cock. She struggled but that enabled her to be more easily spindled on the thumping cock.

"Ouch, that hurts like hell," she hollered.

"The pain will soon disappear," Jet said lying under and in her.

He was right after several minutes the pain diminished and she simply felt a long hard object stuffed up her ass.

Jet rose, grabbed Rachel's breasts, and pulled her onto his chest. Her legs were spread and a cock glided into her pussy.

It felt strange having two staffs deep within her being only a membrane apart, but the feeling changed to pleasure when both men stroked her. Over and over again the two cocks in sync pushed into her and withdrew.

They continued in unison until they both came with shouts, "Yes, yes, yes, oh man that's great!"

As their warm cum filled her orifices she climaxed with them, "Yaaaugh, ooooough, aaaagh, woooow"

Before she had time to think, she was lifted and her asshole impaled on a different spear and her pussy by another cock. Soon she lay in ecstasy of being stroked by two cocks until they emptied their loads into her openings with shouts of pleasure, and she climaxed with them.

The double penetrations continued until all four men had the opportunity to come in her ass and cunt. When they were exhausted they took her to the bathroom bathed, rinsed, and dried her before returning her to a freshly made bed. After she was covered with a sheet and blanket, each of the men stopped to give her a chaste kiss on the lips and thank her for the wonderful time.

The light was turned out as they left. An exhausted and sexually satisfied Rachel slept.

* * *

Rachel sat fatigued but sexually satisfied in her first class seat on the way to Atlanta. She contemplated what to do with the money she'd made and the invitation to return to another writer's workshop. She closed her eyes to reflect on the incredible orgasms she received during the five gangbangs she'd experienced. Smiling to herself she thought of a new aphorism: not enough parties, not enough bars, not enough drinks, but almost enough sex.

Two For Debbie (Threesomes)

Debbie goes to a club hoping for one & gets two

Debbie was getting into dire straights. She was going through batteries in her vibrators like there was no tomorrow. The real problem was that she was horny and while she was getting herself off, there was just nothing like having a real live man between her legs. She couldn't wrap her legs around a vibrator, and it didn't hug her. It didn't talk so it couldn't tell her that she looked nice, felt nice, and smelled nice. While it never complained if she had another vibrator in bed, and she often did these days, and didn't complain if she had a headache, it never kissed her goodnight either.

Even her small collection of adult videos weren't doing anything for her, including the home made ones she was in. They were fond memories, but it wasn't enough. She was going to take care of some of that problem tonight. She was going to church. More correctly, she was going to The Church. It was a former church, and a large one at that, that had been converted into a large nightclub; A huge establishment that had two bands and a disk jockey. It also had one other important item - MEN! Even more important, there was a large assortment of men there.

Debbie had broken up with her last boyfriend over two weeks now. The best part of that relationship had been sex, and that hadn't been that great. He was a little too possessive and conventional - in other words, she had to be on the bottom most of the time. He was also lacking in the oral department, something she loved dearly. Tonight she was going to find a man who was a little more open-minded; just maybe she would be able to find two of them! Debbie had only been in a threesome once. It had been her and two guys, and while it hadn't been all that great (the one guy didn't really get into the spirit of things), she would dearly love to be in another one.

She dressed for the hunt; a skimpy bra, silky thong undies, thigh-high stockings, short dark skirt, a tight fitting knit top that buttoned up the front, and short heels. While she was small breasted, she had come to realize over the last few years that the size of them had little to do with sex appeal for most men. She didn't have an hourglass figure, but that didn't seem to count for much either. She had finally learned that how she carried herself and her attitude was what made her sexy. She looked at herself in the full-length mirror, undid a few of the small buttons on the top to show a little more cleavage, and decided she was a good-looking piece - she was definitely dangerous! She tidied the house up a little before she left. She liked it nice and neat if she was going to bring anyone home, not that most men would really notice.

Phil and Ed were roommates. Neither had a steady girlfriend at the moment, something both of them wanted, but not desperately. They had been desperate before, with disastrous results; both now had very bitchy ex wives. Tonight they were heading off to church - The Church - to do a little praying, praying that they each found a girl to take home, praying that they got laid! They weren't going there to be greedy, two each would be heaven, but one for each of them was more realistic. Since they had been in threesomes together before, if they had to, they would settle for one playful girl that wanted the two of them. They each took a shower, shaved, and then, just in case one or both of them got lucky tonight, they did the unthinkable and cleaned the apartment. They also did the completely unthinkable and put the seat down on the toilet! Their experience had been that a sloppy apartment turned off women.

Just in case they both got lucky tonight, they each drove their own car.

The two men arrived at The Church about eight and were fortunate enough to find a table. It wasn't a front row seat, but rather one in the rear of that particular bar, near the bar itself and away from the speakers. That made talking to and being heard by a woman a lot easier. They weren't here to hear the band; they were here to find someone to take home tonight. This was serious business.

Debbie arrived at The Church a little after nine. She was immediately hit upon by two guys she wanted nothing to do with. Getting away from them hadn't proven to be too difficult, but she was off to a bad start. During the next hour she found several prospects, but quickly had decided that each of them wouldn't do. Hunting for the perfect bedmate tonight wasn't going to be easy. It all seemed easy enough before she got here; just pick up a nice looking hunk, take him home, get screwed silly, and kick him out before he wanted to stay all night. It was just past ten before she ran into her next possibility, Ed.

Ed spotted Debbie at the bar getting another drink. He had introduced himself and asked her to dance. She had accepted his invitation, and after two fast songs and one slow one, he had invited her to Phil and his table. Ed thought if he could woo this one, he had a real winner. He didn't know what the chances of getting into her pants were, but he had taken to her immediately. At least he had a girl to talk to, and that was a lot better than what Phil had at the moment. Poor Phil's eyes had about come out of his head when he brought Debbie back to the table.

Phil was striking out big-time tonight. He was getting rejected by the good looking and acceptable women, and getting hit on by the dogs. Like most bars, this one had its share of dogs. He was getting the sinking feeling that this was going to be a sex free night. He had just come back from his...he had lost count of the number of reject for the night, when Ed had returned to the table with a very hot looking woman in tow. It looked like Ed was going to do okay tonight. Ed introduced Debbie to Phil, and the three sat there talking, and getting to know each other over the next hour.

Phil had excused himself and asked a few other women to dance, but still wasn't getting anywhere. If the woman he was with thought he was okay, there was something about her that had bothered him, and if he thought the woman was okay, she had declined any further dances or invitations. He just wasn't doing too well. Each time he had returned to the table and continued talking to Ed and Debbie. By a little after midnight, the bar crowd was thinning out and the prospects of finding anyone for himself were getting very slim. Ed was probably going home with Debbie, from the sounds of their conversation and the way she was dancing with Ed during the slow dances, and he would be going back to their place alone. While he had had a few drinks, the dogs weren't looking good yet. "Do you happen to have a sister?" he asked Debbie in desperation.

"Sorry, no sisters." Right now Debbie didn't want any either. She decided he was really getting desperate. She was getting along very well with Ed. His buddy Phil was a very nice guy, but he wasn't doing very well when it came to finding someone for himself. She knew they shared a place by now, and was wondering what they thought of threesomes. While she had been sitting at the table, she had managed to get another button undone on her top without anyone noticing her doing it. The top was now open to just above her bra. It had the desired effect. Within a few moments she had Ed's undivided attention and she had seen Phil glancing at her chest more and more.

Unlike her experiences with a lot of men, she felt very comfortable almost immediately with these two men. If there was a time when she felt like doing a threesome with two men she hardly knew, it was now and with these two. It was just a matter of how to bring the subject up and if they would go for it. All too many men wanted very little to do with a woman right after another man had just had her. She also had to broach the subject before Phil managed to find someone for himself; timing was everything. Phil just might get desperate and pick up some girl that was good enough for a one night stand pretty soon and put an end the very idea of a threesome. Debbie had been mulling this over in her mind long enough that she was now wet with anticipation. She had just about worked herself up enough nerve to ask them when Phil, sounding a little rejected, brought the subject up.

"Looks like I have managed to strike out here tonight," he said looking around at the thinning crowd. "Anyone for a threesome? You know, double your fun and all that." he asked, making a joke of it. He thought Ed would be okay with the idea, but he had no idea what Debbie was going to do. It was probably going to be yet another rejection for the night. He just hoped he hadn't blown it for Ed if she was really turned off by the idea.

"I've done it before," Debbie quipped, rather surprising herself with her quick answer. Christ, her hormones were taking control! Now she really hoped that she hadn't scared off her one good prospect for getting laid tonight. As soon as she had said it, she wished she hadn't opened her big mouth. Phil was probably just kidding, and she still had no idea what Ed thought of threesomes.

"So have we," Ed said. "Not often, but every now and then we run into a girl who gets into being satisfied by two men."

"Yea," Phil piped up, "but for some reason they are always about to get married or it turns out they are cheating on some guy who's knuckles drag on the ground and he used to play defensive line for the NFL."

"We've really been able to pick 'em," Ed said with a sigh. "That last guy really put a new slant on football."

Her prayers had been answered. It must have been some leftover karma from the church. All she had to do was play her cards right and these two were hers for the evening. "Well," she started, "I can assure that I'm not married and have no boyfriend at the moment."

"Are you serious about a threesome with the two of us?" Ed asked. He liked nice wet sloppy sex. While he had hoped to have her for himself earlier, he was really getting turned on to the idea of a threesome with her.

"Sure. You two strike me as two guys I could really have a great time with."

"In that case," Ed said, "your place or ours?"

"You two must be as horny as I am," she said with a giggle. "How about mine? I have a nice king-sized bed." She really wasn't going to risk spoiling this by going to their place. After all, two single guys living together? Get real! She didn't really want to know how bad that place looked.

"There is no longer any point in hanging around here," said Phil standing up. "Let's go party!"

The three left. Debbie led the caravan to her place. She was almost too giddy to drive. Boy was she going to get it tonight! She went to The Church hoping to find one decent looking horny guy and was now going home with two. Even better, these Phil and Ed and done threesomes before so there wouldn't be any surprises like the last time. That threesome had gone well until the first guy had come in her. The other guy wanted nothing to do with her after that, other than another blowjob. Blowjobs might have been nice for him, but they didn't exactly get her off. These two apparently had no such qualms and from the way they were talking at The Church, they actually liked a "used" woman. Debbie hoped they would "use" her a lot tonight.

The trio arrived at Debbie's place without anyone getting lost. In the living room, the two men sat on the couch, unsure just how she wanted to get started, or if she had changed her mind about a threesome for that matter.

"So," she said standing in front of them, "are you two a little shy about getting undressed, or am I supposed to do a strip for you first?"

"Uh.a nice slow strip would be nice!" quipped Phil. "Got any beer?" Might as well take full advantage of the amenities. If she was willing to strip for them, he was sure willing to watch not that he really needed to get any hornier than he already was. She could have suggested that they just head for the bedroom, and that would have worked for him.

"That would be nice," Ed chimed in. "but we could just head..."

"Just shut up and watch!" Phil said as he elbowed Ed. "I don't find women that want to do a strip too often. Come to think of it, I don't think I ever have."

Debbie got the two guys a couple of beers. She didn't normally drink the stuff, but she kept it around for times like this. She put on a CD that she thought would be good for a little stripping. If it was a show they wanted, then it would be a show they would get. Debbie had a pretty good idea of how to do a decent strip tease and while she had never thought of doing it, that little off-hand remark now sounded like a pretty good idea. She was a bit of a showoff, and with this small audience, it just might be fun. As the music started she started slowly dancing by herself. As she danced, she began to unbutton her top.

The whole idea of a strip was to get them very excited, she did it slowly. When all the buttons were finally undone, she twirled around a few times before letting it slide off her arms to the floor. The skirt was next. There wasn't much too that, just a button at the top and a zipper. Undoing the button didn't do much, and was the zipper went down the skirt immediately began to slide down over her hips. With the zipper all the way down, all she had to do was let go of it and the skirt joined the blouse on the floor. Debbie felt very sexy and more than just a little risque, dancing in her skimpy undies and bra. From the squirming the two men were doing and from the bulges in their pants, she was having the desired affect.

Ed and Phil sat and watched Debbie, too entranced to even drink their beers. They just held them and watched her. She wasn't a runway model, but she had their undivided attention.

Of all of the girlfriends Ed had had, none was ever willing do put on a show like this. The last one hadn't been too fond of getting undressed in front of him for that matter. She liked sex all right, but she thought it ought to be done with the lights out. She had loved to be eaten and gave a very nice blowjob, but sex with the lights on was just something she wasn't too fond of. Doing a strip for him and his buddy was out of the question. Now here they sat on a girl's couch, one they hardly knew, and she was doing a very seductive strip tease for them!

Phil had a few rowdy girlfriends in his time, but he had never had one willing to stand up with all the lights in the house on and strip for two guys she had just met. He had a few that were into threesomes, but it was only after they got to know him and whoever it was that was going to be the third person that they had been willing to take anything off.

The music continued and Debbie finally undid the snap on her front closing bra. Her breasts were firm enough that while the snap was undone; they didn't allow the bra to just fall off her either. Her breasts separated a little, but the nipples remained covered. After leaving the two guys to wonder if that damn thing was ever going to come off, she finally peeled it off her breasts and it joined the skirt and blouse on the floor. She was so excited now that her nipples were sticking out like someone had been sucking on them. She danced very close to the two guys now just to make sure they had a very good look at them. Now, she turned around, bent over and slid her thong undies down her sexy legs, giving the two guys a very up-close and personal look at her ass as she did it. They never said a word; they were speechless. "So guys, what do you think?" she said moving away a little and turning around.

"I think you have a very sexy body and we're over dressed!" said Phil.

"We can fix that," said Ed getting up.

"I certainly hope so," Debbie said as she picked up her clothes. "Because I'm going to the bedroom now, and I don't want anyone in there dressed, that's for sure." She walked into her bedroom, picked up a TV-like remote control on the bed, pushed a button on it, and then put it in her nightstand drawer. Now she dropped her clothes on a chair and pulled the covers back on her bed. Before she was done there were two naked men in the room helping her.

Ed was hard and ready for her. He didn't care if he was first of second or which end of her he got to put it in her, just as long as he got to. He thought Debbie was going to be a pretty hot little number when he had first started taking to her back at The Church, but this was way beyond his dreams. Girls like this were something he read about, but never got.

Phil had wanted a girl of his own earlier. Now he was rather happy to be here with Debbie and Ed. This evening was off to a very good start. Just the thought of a hot wet messy threesome with her had gotten him all nice and hard. He couldn't wait to get into her.

The three crawled to the center of Debbie's king-sized bed. She stayed on all fours and began to suck on the nearest one to her head, Ed. He was nicely equipped, not too big, and very hard. She took him into her mouth and began to give him the best blowjob she could.

For a few short seconds, Ed thought he was going to come in her mouth as soon as she took him into it. Debbie's mouth was hot and wet, and she sure had a talented tongue! It was hard to believe things had moved this fast tonight. Usually getting a girl in bed on the first date was somewhere between hard and impossible, and here he was having a threesome with Debbie!

Phil wasted no time moving around to Debbie's hot little rear. It was going to be difficult to eat her in this position, but he craned his neck and did as good as he could. Apparently she liked what he was doing as she was moaning some even while she had Ed stuck into her mouth about as far as he had ever seen a woman take a man. Whatever she was doing to Ed, it must have been good, as he had his head back and his eyes were closed. Phil finally gave up trying to eat Debbie in this position and decided it was just time to take her doggie style. He moved into position, slid his hard cock up and down between her very wet sex lips, and slid all the way into her. He couldn't believe how wet and tight she was. She must have been just about as horny as he was, from the sound of the moan she let out when he grabbed her hips and pushed himself into her as far as he could go.

"Sounds like you're making her feel good," Ed said. "You realize of course that you're wreckin' this blowjob. She's finding it a little hard to concentrate I'm afraid."

"Sorry pal," Phil said as he pumped away at Debbie, "this is too good to wait till you're done."

"Sorry Ed," Debbie said as his hard shaft slid out of her mouth. "I can't blow you and get fucked by Phil at the same time. He isn't being too gentle back there and it's moving me around too much and...I'm...going to come soon, and I need this badly!"

"No problem," he said reaching under her and fondling her breast. "I just hope you are the multi-orgasmic kind so you can get off again when I take over from Phil. From the sound of his breathing I don't think he can last long either."

"I am...Oh Jesus, I'm coming!" she groaned as her orgasm started.

Debbie had no sooner started coming than Phil felt the first load of his come start up his shaft and erupt into Debbie. Spurt after spurt of his hot come rushed into her climaxing body. He was horny and gave her all he had. Poor Ed, he thought, he just has to sit on the sidelines while I fill what was going to be his date with all the come I have in me.

"Poor Ed" wasn't feeling the least bit sorry for himself. He was now toying with Debbie's nipples as she came, pinching and pulling on them, and just waiting for his turn with her. He hadn't had a nice sloppy sex session in a long time, and tonight he was looking forward to this one! He just hoped he didn't get too excited when he got to slide into her very wet pussy and shoot his stuff too soon.

It was over all too soon for Phil. That was the trouble with actually coming. Too bad it didn't last a lot longer, he thought, but then maybe if it did he would have a heat attack it felt so good. As comes go this had been a pretty good one. He stayed inside Debbie as she came down off hers, enjoying the squeezes her pussy gave him from time to time. "Looks like it's about your turn Ed," he said as he finally pulled out. He noticed a large gob of come run out of her when he pulled out. She was just so tight there wasn't room for all that come in her.

"I'm ready for more," Debbie said, "but I think I want to be on my back this time." As Phil got out of the way, she rolled over onto her back, changed her position on the bed a little, and spread her legs for Ed. "Come and get it," she said still breathing hard. "Jesus Phil, sorta gave me a little come didn't you? It's running down my ass!"

"The flood hasn't begun," Ed said getting between her legs. "If you want to see a flood, just wait a few minutes." He aimed his hard cock at her sopping wet pussy and plunged all the way into her, feeling the fresh come on him. There was so much of it that he almost immediately felt his balls getting wet from it. This was every bit as delicious as he had fondly remembered the last time he had done this. This felt so good that he had to hold still with his cock in her as far as he could shove it. For a few seconds he thought he was going to blow it and come just from the feeling of her come soaked pussy grasping him. After he calmed down, he began moving in and out of Debbie, slowly as first, then picking up the speed as he got closer to coming. He was sitting up between Debbie's legs as he pumped away at her. He would love to lie right down on her and feel her hot body against his, but he had to give Phil access to those great tits of her.

Debbie loved every minute of this. She had gotten off once tonight and she was quickly on her way to coming again. He bottom was very wet now, and Ed pumping away at her was making hot sexy squishing sounds as their bodies met. Ed was forcing the last of Phil's love juices of her and they were running down her ass and onto the bed. This was one night where she didn't care how big the wet spot got. She was holding Phil's still hard shaft in her hand and pumping away at it as much as she could. He was playing with her sensitive nipples while Ed was having her, pulling, pinching, and twisting them. This was sheer heaven.

Phil was up by Debbie's head, and while he had hoped that she would blow him while Ed was having her, he soon realized that even though she was on her back, she would have the same problem that she had trying to blow Ed when he was inside her. Ed was holding Debbie's hips now and pounding away at her, causing her to move around on the bed almost as much had he had made her when he had her doggie style. She was also moaning and groaning so much that he doubted she would be able to blow him anyway. He was surprised that he was still hard after unloading in her like he had, but her hot little hand was doing its best to keep him in his current state. What Phil really wanted to do now was slide back into Debbie just as soon as Ed was done. Maybe that's what was really keeping him so hard. He hoped she was up to it. From the sounds the two were making, he wouldn't have to wait long.

Ed was hoping Debbie would come soon, as it was all he could do to not come himself by now. This was so hot and wet. As if Debbie had read his mind, she started coming. There was a loud groan from her and he felt her body start to jerk and heave with her orgasm. That was all it took. He grabbed her hips and pulled her firmly to him as his first huge spurt of come raced up his hard shaft and erupted deep inside her coming body. Spurt after spurt followed the first one. This was a great come, it lasted and lasted. He knew he hadn't been exaggerating when he told Phil that the flood of come coming out of her when Phil was done with her was nothing compared to what he was going to give her. It felt like he was pumping gallons of his come into her.

Debbie was enjoying this second orgasm of the night. It wasn't as strong as the first one had been, but it was nice nonetheless. She could feel Ed's firm cock throbbing deep inside her as he filled her. It was a wonderful feeling - and it was sure making a mess down there! The poor guy was trying to pump for her, not that he really needed to, but he was coming so hard it was all he could do just to hang on to her. She loved knowing it was her hot body that was making him come that much.

When the two were finally done, Phil was still hard and still very anxious to get back inside Debbie now that Ed had filled her. He, like Ed, loved hot wet messy sex. Just the thought of being inside a woman who had just been with another man was enough to get him hard, and now he was about to have the real thing. "Are you up to another one?" he asked her as Ed pulled out of her.

"Yea, I guess so," she said still breathing hard. "I guess I can come again."

"God I'm going to love this!" Phil said taking Ed's place.

"You guys really get into this kind of sex don't you?" Debbie asked as she raised her ass up off the bed a little.

"Just a little." Phil said softly as he aimed himself at Debbie's very wet bottom. There was a river of come running out of her now; the remnants of his first load, Ed's come, and some of Debbie's sex juices. Phil slid the head of his cock around Debbie's pussy opening, getting it all wet with the come, before shoving it slowly into her. Unlike Ed, he didn't plunge right into her, but took his time sliding slowly into her as he savored the feeling of her come soaked pussy slowly moving up his hard shaft.

"Do you like the feeling?" she asked, noticing that he was taking his time entering her.

"Oh do I ever. This is so hot!"

"I like being had by more that one guy, but I never understood what was in it for the guys."

"Beats me," Phil said as he began to pump away at her. "Some shrink would probably tell you I'm nuts, but I just know it really turns me on."

"Same here," volunteered Ed as he sat next to her. "I just know it's really hot."

Phil was starting to pump faster now. He wasn't in any too big a hurry, having gotten off once already this evening, but he knew Debbie would be getting sore if he didn't hurry a little.

Debbie was surprised to find her third come of the evening coming on so quickly. Phil just felt good inside her. She put a finger on her clit just to speed things along. Ed was carefully playing with her nipples and apparently knew that they would be getting a little tender by now. It wouldn't be long before she got off again.

Phil was in heaven. There was come dripping off his balls and his pubic hair was soaking wet with come. In spite of all the lubrication and having been laid twice, Debbie was surprisingly tight. He was getting ready to come again. "I hope you're getting close," he said softly.

"Real close," she whispered. "Go ahead and come if you want."

Phil wanted to. He gave her a few more hard pumps, going all the way into her, and felt the first load of come start up from deep down in his balls. "Oh God, here it comes," he groaned. He felt her give him a good hard squeeze as the first load shot into her. He had another great come, pumping load after load of come deep into her. He wasn't sure how much he was really giving her after emptying his balls into her once already, but it sure felt like it was a lot. Just after he had started, he felt her start to come.

"I'm coming!" Debbie screamed. She had been close when she felt Phil's cock swell a little and start to twitch inside her as he started coming. That was all it took to send her over the edge. It was a lot better one than she thought she would have.

When Debbie was done, Phil let his now softening cock slide out of her. It, and the area surrounding it, was covered with a thick wet layer of come. He was a mess!

"How do you feel about doing it one more time?" Ed asked her.

"I don't know. I think I would get pretty sore, even as slick as I am. How about if I just blow you?"

"Uh...sure." How could he pass that up? He thought her time with Phil might have been the last, but this sure beat nothing.

Debbie rolled over onto her stomach now and moved over to where Ed was crouched. She also moved out of that huge wet spot she had been lying in. She gave his hard cock a few strokes with her hand before taking him into her mouth. After a few short in and out strokes, she was taking Ed deep into her mouth and almost into her throat.

"That feels great," he said softly, "really great."

Debbie just kept working on him. In and out that rigid cock went. She paid special attention to the sensitive underside of the head when only the head remained in her mouth. It was getting late and she didn't want to make this a long protracted blowjob. She knew exactly what to do to get him off, and she was good at it. One hand followed her mouth up and down his rigid shaft. The other hand firmly cupped his balls. It wasn't very long until she had him about ready to come.

"Oh Jesus, I'm about ready to come," he warned her. He didn't know if she wanted his next load of come in her mouth, but he thought he would warn her. Debbie kept right on sucking on him. A few more nice deep into-her-throat sucks and Ed was going over the edge. "Here is comes," he groaned as a last warning, not that it was much of a warning, as the first spurt of come rushed up his shaft and into her waiting mouth. She kept right on working on him as he pumped spurt after spurt of come into her mouth and down her throat. He felt like she was sucking him dry. When he was finally done, she let his softening cock slip from her mouth. Not a drop of his come had escaped her mouth.

"Well guys," she said finally. "I hate to shove you out the door, but I need a little sleep as I have to get up in the morning."

Ed and Phil got dressed and got ready to go. It had been one hot night, but each was looking forward to a good nights sleep - or what was left of the night - in their own bed. Three in one bed just didn't cut it. They had tried that trick too. The each gave her a nice wet kiss before going out the door.

When they were safely gone, Debbie raced back to the bedroom, opened her partly opened closet door all the way, and checked on her video camera. The tape had run out and it was just sitting there dark and quiet. Now, if it had just lasted as long enough to catch her blowing Ed; she pushed the rewind button.

Anal Sex and Trust (Anal Sex)

A gentle story about 1st time anal sex.

Alex had Devin pinned on the bed, finally! Her long slender legs were pinned between his, and he held her arms above her head by her wrists. He looked down at the woman beneath him. She lay flat on her back with her hair wild all around her head on the pillow, almost like a halo. Her face flushed a pretty shade of pink, her eyes dancing with mischief, and a stunning smile on her lips. Alex's eyes slid lower, down her neck to her chest; she was still breathing hard trying to catch her breath from laughing so hard. Her nipples pressed hard against her thin pink tank top.

"I got you!" Alex taunted playfully.

"Not fair! You cheated!" Devin giggled.

"How do you figure?" Alex slowly released Devin's hands but she left them to rest above her head. She did not seem to mind all that much being pinned. Slowly he traced a finger down the side of her delicate face, along her jaw, down her neck, and then gently down into the dip of her tank top. He watched her crystal blue eyes closely, seeing the mischief swiftly replaced with desire. "Well Devin, how did I cheat?"

"I..I...don't recall." Devin said softly. She gasped when his fingers found one pert little nipple and tweaked it carefully.

Alex reached down between them and pushed her tank top up over her breasts, fully exposing them to his eyes and hands. She watched him, but kept her hands relaxed above her head. Her cheeks were still flushed. Alex thought that she looked like an angel before him. He shifted down slowly to bring his lips to hers. There was no hesitation, Devin parted her lips and the kiss took on its own life. Everything else sunk away, it was just the two of them. Her breathing increased again as his hands roamed over her body. Finally she brought her hands to his head and held him as they kissed with a fevered passion. It was always like this for them, as soon as their lips met it elevated them to another place where just they existed.

Alex broke the kiss, leaving them both breathless. He rained small kisses down the path his finger had taken just minutes before, across her jaw, down her neck to her chest where he took one perfect pink nipple into his mouth and sucked on it. A small sweet sound escaped Devin's slightly parted lips. With a butterfly light touch she caressed his face, neck, and shoulders. She watched him still, just enthralled with the man before her. It made her heart skip a beat every single time he touched her. Even the most innocent of touches had such a strong affect on her.

He felt her body tremble as she slid his lips and tongue down her smooth stomach and stopped just above the top of her lace black thong. He kissed her tenderly as he ran his hands over her thighs. She felt so very soft, and her scent so very feminine. She was quite simply intoxicating to him. No matter how much she willingly offered him, he always wanted more. He could not seem to ever have enough of her, even when he was buried deeply within her while they made love. Tucking his fingers into the sides of her thong he lowered it ever so slightly, kissing the newly exposed flesh. He watched goose bumps rise on her skin. Soft moans slipped unchecked from her lips. She whispered his name and gasped as he pulled the thong down, more fully exposing her

Devin watched Alex with heavy desire coursing through her body. No man's touch had ever had this level of effect on her before. She was not sure how they could have been tickling and play-fighting just a few minutes before, to being this aroused and this needy now. She could not quite figure it out, but it did not matter. She wanted him, and she could see at the stunning bulge in his boxers that he wanted her. His mouth was hovering just above her pussy. Every nerve in her body felt as if it is exploding under his kisses and touches, as well as the anticipation of what was to follow. Moans and gasps escape her mouth without her even intending them.

She almost groaned as Alex lifted himself off the bed. He quickly pulled her panties down her legs and off, before he removed his boxers, and returned to her side. She licked her lips looking at his naked form. His erection was thick and very hard. She felt her body temperature ratchet up several notches. He carefully parted her thighs and she bit her lower lip. Alex delved his fingers into her moist folds, caressing her and finding all of her most magical places. She looked to his face and saw his heavy desires written there. She felt him push a finger into her body, and her back arched from the bed. She was at his mercy, and they both knew it.

Heat ripped through her entire body as Alex replaced his fingers with his mouth. Tasting and exploring her with his mouth. He positioned himself between her widely spread thighs. She looked down at him with heavily hooded eyes. She smiled lovingly when he glanced up at her. She was not sure which one of them was enjoying this more. Her pulse raced as she threw her head back and simply allowed the sensations to wash over her. She could hear her heart pounding in her ears, and within no time she felt the amazing waves of an orgasm wash over her and through her. Her body shook with her release, but Alex did not let her relax. Instead he pushed two fingers into her and slowly began to kiss his way back up her body.

Their lips met again. Without hesitation she opened her mouth and pushed her tongue into his. They kissed wildly and with pure abandon, exploring each other's mouths fully and sharing her taste. Alex kept his fingers buried within her. She could sense the urgency within him, and she felt it too. Devin pulled her lips from his, and looked into his eyes. She bit her lower lip, almost nervously.

"What is it, baby? Is everything okay?" Alex asked, concerned now.

"Yeah, I mean yes. Everything is fine. I was just thinking that maybe we could..." Her face flushed more, even though that hardly seemed possible.

"Babes, you can ask me anything. Don't be scared."

"We bought the lubricant, and I thought maybe you might want to try..." Her voice trailed off again, but Alex did not need to hear the res t. He knew what she was suggesting. He smiled softly at her, hoping to ease her shyness. Alex knew she was suggesting that they have anal sex, and the very idea made him crazy with lust, but he was also was nervous of hurting her.

"Are you sure you want it?" He asked cautiously. He had to be sure she wanted it for her and not to please him. She nodded very deliberately. He could see conviction in her pretty blue eyes. He felt his manhood throb.

She rolled swiftly onto her stomach. He looked down at her perfectly cute little bottom. He had to touch it, so he allowed his hands to explore first and then his lips at he placed sweet kisses on her smooth cheeks. He heard her reach into the bedside table. His heart beat quickened. She passed him the tube of lubricant. He took it feeling almost sheepish. He wanted this very much, but still felt unsure about what was in it for her.

When he hesitated a few moments too long, she gently took charge.

She sat up and spun to face him. "This is going to be good and enjoyable for us both, please trust me." She looked into his eyes and he believed her.

He watched as Devin took the lubricant from his hands and squeezed and generous amount onto her hand. She reached for his hard cock. Her hand was warm and snug over him as she thoroughly spread the slick gel over him. It felt incredibly good, and then she stopped and handed him back the tube. "Now, I did you so you have to do me." She winked and quickly got onto all fours on the bed. He has a perfect view of her bum, and her pussy nestled between her thighs. His mouth went dry, and all other thoughts left his head. He could only think about her and being with her in this naughty way. He moved behind her, kneeling there. Opening the tube of lubricant he squeezed a good amount onto his fingers. He slid his fingers between her rounded cheeks and spread the gel over her. She made a soft sound. She was clearly into what they were about to do. His cock throbbed harder. He reached out and massaged her hips, pressing his hard cock lengthwise into her crack. He just touched her for a full minute, before finally taking his cock in his hand and pressing the head to her back entrance.

One of them trembled. Maybe both, he could not be sure. He pushed a little at her entrance, but her body resisted. Taking one of her hips with one hand, he used the other to guide his cock. He pressed a little harder, and felt the resistance give and the head of his cock slide inside her. She made a small slightly startled sound, but it sounded more to be of pleasure than pain. Alex tried to get his ragged breathing back under control. That was an impossible feat, as Devin pressed back ever so slightly encouraging him.

"Devin..." Alex managed to say through clenched teeth.

"Mmmhmm." Devin almost moaned.

She sounded like she was enjoying herself, but the protector in him pressed him to ask. "Will you stop me if it hurts you?"

"Yes Alex! Now please..."

Alex did not need any further reassuring. Taking hold of both of her hips now, he pushed slowly into her until he was buried as deeply as he dared. Again he paused, as much for her as for himself. She was incredibly tight around him. It was very different from her pussy, but very good. Almost too good, and almost too tight, he thought. Gently he eased himself back a few inches and then pushed back into her. She moaned a little louder now. Perspiration beaded on her fair skin. She glanced over her shoulder and looked deeply into his eyes. The lust in her eyes was unmistakable. She was enjoying herself, and he did not see an ounce of discomfort.

Slowly he built a gentle rhythm, taking longer strokes in and out of her. He watched as she reached underneath herself and used her fingers to massage her clit. Alex knew that he could not last all that long. He pushed into her back end again and again. It seemingly had loosened ever so slightly, but was still impossibly too tight. Her body clasped him so tightly, and her moaning and delicate grunts filled his ears. He was sure he was about to cum, when Devin suddenly went off. Her orgasm came over her rapidly, and she cried out calling his name until it blended into one long and erotic moan. Her back end grasped him so tightly, that he could not have held back his need for climax if he tried.

Taking her hips he pushed as deeply into her as their bodies would allow. He was far less careful with her, but in no frame of mind to notice. She gave no indication of being bothered. He made a few more strokes into her before spilling his cum deeply into her with a loud guttural moan of his own. His head felt light, and his body also covered with sweat. He stayed there behind her for almost a full minute before he could process a thought. When he could think again, he ever so gingerly eased himself out of her. He watched as Devin gently lowered her perfect body to the bed and turned her head to look at him.

Alex wasted no time lowering his body down beside her, snuggling close, and putting his strong arms around her. She turned her head to look into his eyes again. She had the most blissful smile on her lips. Alex could not help but smile back at her. What they had just done had been incredible, but the trust she had put in him had been even more amazing to him.

"Thank you." He whispered, reaching over to tuck some of her hair behind her ear.

"Thank you." She answered softly.

No Tell Motel (Taboo Sex)

Siblings take their relationship into the taboo.

***

"Well here we are," Noah said sitting behind the wheel of his truck, as they both sat looking at the front of the motel.

"Yep," Holly answered softly.

The two sat in awkward silence, Noah wringing the steering wheel as Holly fidgeted with the straps of her purse.

"This is so crazy," Holly finally broke the silence. She looked around the outside of the motel, the ugly tan door of one of the rooms directly in front of Noah's truck. "I'm sitting in my brother's truck at some sleazy no tell motel because he wants to have sex with his sister." The parking lot was mostly empty, not a surprise for a weekday afternoon. She was not sure if an empty parking lot was good or bad, fewer people meant they would be more noticeable to anyone who would look, but it also meant a lower risk of being seen by some one that knew them.

"I know, I never thought I'd actually be in this situation."

"But you hoped, huh?" She turned toward him with a smile.

"Hell yes, just never thought there was a way for it to happen, not in my wildest dreams."

"Oh I think you did a lot more than sit in a truck with me in your wildest dreams," her grin widened.

"Umm ... well, okay you got me there."

"I should have freaked out. I should have slapped you, or cursed you, or ... just left," she said.

"But you didn't."

"I didn't did I ... why is that?"

"You tell me, you didn't freak and then you came here."

She took a deep breath, "I haven't a clue Noah ... curiosity maybe."

"Curiosity?"

"Curious about what it would be like, if I could do it, how far I could go," she looked at him arching an eyebrow, "how much fun it might be."

He turned to meet her gaze, "too much fun is my guess."

"Pervert," she slapped his arm.

"Obviously."

"I know I said this before, but I can't guarantee how far I can go. If I can do anything. No promises about what might happen in there."

"I know. I'm just glad you're here ... with me."

"I am here," she looked at the door to the motel again. "But I know nothing will happen in the parking lot. Want to go in?"

"God yes."

She giggled, "you must be really excited."

"I feel like I'm going to burst."

"I thought I was supposed to make you do that?" She smiled mischievously.

"Tease," he said.

"You haven't seen anything yet."

He gulped as he stared at her, she was so beautiful, her lithe fit body, toned from years of running, tennis, and cheerleading. Her long blonde hair curled around her shoulders. She had been the object of his deepest sexual fantasies for as long as he could remember, and now she was sitting next to him, in front of a motel. He was so close to his ultimate fantasy he could hardly contain his excitement.

"Let's get inside," she said as she opened the door of the truck and stepped out into the humid air and heat of the parking lot. "I hope the air conditioning works in there, it's so hot."

"You're hot."

"Am I?" She smiled as they walked toward the door of the motel, "or are you just saying that hoping you'll get lucky?"

"Both, but mostly just the first one," he said as he opened the motel door. The room was gloomy, thick curtains hung half open over the room's only window. Any hope for relief from the heat vanished instantly, it was oppressively hot inside. He watched his sister cross the room, her ass swaying in her tight denim shorts. She set her purse down on the small table that sat in the far corner. She took a minute to check the curtains, making sure they were pulled tight.

"There we go," she said, "don't want anyone getting a look inside do we."

"Probably not," he grinned as she walked up to him where he stood between the two beds.

"This is too weird isn't it?" I keep thinking it'll get easier but it doesn't."

"You want to leave?"

"No," she looked up at him smiling at hearing the obvious disappointment in his voice. "I'm just conflicted, confused ... it's exciting too though, ya know?"

"It's taboo, I think that's a big part of it."

"Yeah, it's really wrong, and yet ... it's turning me on."

"Is it?"

"It is, I'm scared and I have to confess, getting a bit wet."

"Oh god," he groaned.

"Like that huh?"

"You're so hot Holly," he said as he admired his sister, standing before him in her small denim shorts that showed off her slender tanned legs and her thin button up pink shirt, she was a fan of pink. She had left the top few buttons undone, her ample round breasts on display, beats of sweat collected across her skin, running down the valley of her cleavage.

"So you keep saying."

"Don't believe me?"

She took a step toward him, their bodies almost touching, "umm, no your excitement is pretty obvious. Your cock has been hard this whole time."

"Ugh," he groaned.

"What like I wouldn't notice that," she whispered as she closed the space between them, her large soft breasts pressed to against his chest. Her hands began to run slowly across his chest.

"It's the idea of who noticed it."

"Yeah, because I'm not supposed to notice am I? Good girls don't look at their little brother's big hard cocks."

"Fuck Holly."

"Maybe you will," she said as she wrapped her arms around his neck, his hands went to her hips. "I really have no idea how far this should go Noah. I mean this is the sort of thing that can't be undone, whatever we do is permanent, we can't go back."

"I know."

"You sure about that, it's not just your hard cock draining blood away from your brain making you say that?"

"Holly I've dreamt about this for years, it won't change anything between us."

"Nothing?"

"Well nothing bad, we'll know each other better, be closer."

"Closer than we should."

"Close as we want ... no one will know."

"No one can know Noah ... no one ... ever. Not a friend on a drunken night, not your girlfriend, not a future wife, not a shrink, no one. This has to stay between us and only us."

"I know Holly ..."

"Being secret makes it hot though doesn't it?"

"That and it being you."

"Listen to you, silver tongued devil," she lifted her face toward his. "Kiss me Noah," she whispered. He leaned down, their lips met for the first time. The siblings kissed softly, their tongues exploring each other as they enjoyed their first taboo contact. Noah's hand slid down and grasped his sister's firm ass, giving it a squeeze, pulling her against him. She pressed her hips forward against her brother, feeling his hardness against her belly. "Wow Noah, that was hot."

"Oh shit Holly."

"I just realized, I am the only way you could ever live out your fantasy aren't I? I'm your only sister, so it's me or nothing huh? If I were to turn and leave you'd be stuck... "

"With the worst case of blue balls the world has ever known."

Holly laughed at that, and then pressed her body to her brother, feeling his hard cock against her once more, "good news bro ... I'm not leaving."

"No?"

"I can't believe I'm here in a motel room with my brother and actually considering committing an incestuous act with him, but here I am. Besides now I have my own problem." She smiled a wicked grin at him, her eyes filled with lust. "My pussy is on fire and she needs attention," she leaned forward, softly kissing his neck and chin as his hands cupped her ass. "Mmmhh," she groaned as he squeezed her firm ass lifting her onto her toes. "What do ya say brother of mine, want to help your sister with her wet pussy?"

"Fuck yes I do."

"Jack will be at work for a few hours yet, so I'm all yours." Noah cupped his sister's firm ass in both hands, lifting her to his level. She immediately wrapped her legs around him as they began to kiss, passionately, their tongues entwined with the heat of a taboo act most wouldn't understand. Holly didn't understand it either really, but she knew in that moment, she wanted her brother more than anything.

Holly unwrapped her legs from her brother, standing again before him. Her hands grabbing handfuls of his shirt pulled it up as it clung to his sweaty body, pausing their kissing just long enough to get it over his head. She slid her hands down his naked chest as she caressed his muscles, feeling the definition. Her hands glided down over his abs, his belt, finally resting on the bulge in his jeans. She felt her brother's thickness for the first time as she gave his cock a squeeze. As she felt her brother in her hand he fumbled hurriedly as he unfastened the buttons of her shirt, exposing her blue cotton bra and ample cleavage.

"Your cock is so hard Noah," she whispered as he began to kiss her neck, her hands rubbing his length through the denim.

"I love your tits," he said as he buried his face in her cleavage smothering her beast flesh in kisses.

Suddenly Noah dropped to his knees in front of her. He unclasped her shorts, pulling the zipper down exposing her panties and the Supergirl emblem emblazoned across his sister's mound.

"Supergirl eh?"

"Oh yeah, forgot I had those on ... cute huh?"

"Very, I'll never look at her the same way again," he said as he kissed the logo.

"Ooh, Noah." She said as she ran her hands through his hair, her hips beginning to rock up and down against his nose, as her shorts fell, wadding up around her ankles.

"Supergirl is my new favorite super hero, but she has to go," he told her as his hands griped the waist band of her panties and pulled.

She felt a bolt of excitement shoot through her as she felt the cotton fabric slide down her hips, her pussy about to be bared to Noah, her baby brother. "Ohh my god Noah ... soo wrong." She looked down at him as her panties joined her shorts in a pile at her ankles. Noah had a direct view of her pussy, his nose inches away as he kneeled in front of her.

"Holy shit Holly."

"You like?"

"Fuckin' perfect."

"Shut up."

"Dead serious, prettiest pussy ever sis."

"Ohh my god, my brother likes my pussy ... I'm going to hell," she said as she tossed her head back, her blond hair cascading down her back as her brother planted a kiss on the small patch of pubic hair she kept trimmed in a small heart shape, an idea her fiancé had suggested. Another bolt of excitement went through her as she thought about Jack. He was at work, having a normal day while she was in a motel room, naked with her brother kissing the most intimate part of her body. She had never cheated before and now she was about to cross that line ... with her baby brother of all people. The thought nearly sent her to orgasm.

Suddenly she felt an arm run between her thighs and a hand grasp her bare ass. Noah lifted her in a quick movement as he stood. She grabbed a hold of him as her swung her to a bed, dropping her onto her back with him on top of her, ankles still bound by her shorts and panties. Their lips met again as their bodies came together.

"Mmm Noah," she groaned as her hands slid down his body. She fumbled with his belt, her hands shaking with excitement. "Up ... up," she moaned. "Stand up for a minute, your fucking belt is being a bastard."

"You're just not very good at belts I think," he said smiling at his sister.

Holly sat up, her denim and cotton bound feet resting on the floor, her brother standing in front of her with his belt half undone and a very large bulge straining to escape its prison. "Maybe," she said as she looked up at him, "take it off and I might show you how I am at cocks." Her eyes widened as she watched her brother peel off his belt in a second, throwing it across the room. "Oh my," she said in her naughtiest voice, as she bit her lip. Her eyes fixed on Noah's hands as he reached for the button of his jeans. "Wait," she stopped him, "let me."

"Yeah?"

"I wanna take it out," she said as she starred at the lump in his pants. "Can I ... pretty please?"

"Fuck yes," he groaned.

Her hands went to his fly, unclasping and lowering the zipper in a swift movement.

"Pretty efficient with that Holly, something I should know?"

"I dunno," Holly answered as she pulled his jeans down over his hips, pilling them up around his ankles like her shorts were around hers, the shape of his hard cock now clearly visible straining against his underwear. "There is a pretty good chance that I like to suck cock."

"Don't tease Holly."

"Oh I'm not teasing, baby brother. I love to suck a big hard dick," she said as she began to pull down the cotton prison that restrained her prize. Her mind again flashed back to Jack and how often she gave him head. She loved it, the feeling of a hard cock in her mouth, the control it gave her, it was power and it made her incredibly hot. "Ohh Noah," she groaned as his cock came into view.

"What?"

"I fucking love your cock," she said in a whisper as she starred at her brother's cock, inches away from her. "My brother's cock ... right here. I wanna play with it Noah, I really do."

"Fuck you tease Holly, you're killing me."

Holly giggled when she heard the desperation in his voice. "I kinda am teasing aren't I?"

"Fuck yes you are."

"Aww, poor baby brother, how can I make it right?"

"Touch it, do something with it."

She put her finger to her chin as if in deep thought. "I suppose I could put it in my mouth."

"Damnit Holly."

"Is that what you want Noah? You want your big sister to wrap her lips around your big hard cock and bob up and down on it?"

"Fuckin killing me."

"Ask me nice, you never know."

"For the love of god ... suck my dick sis."

"I guess, since it's here and all," she said as if she could care less about what they were about to do. In truth she couldn't wait any longer, sitting there with her brother's cock inches away from her, with the reality of such a taboo act so close, there was no way she would be able to resist, she had to have him.

"Fuuuckk," he groaned as he felt her hands touch his cock.

"Oh god Noah," she said feeling the hardness of his cock against her hand as she slid it up the length of his cock, the skin soft, the veins ... she needed it. She had entered the room unsure about what might happen, if anything. She had thought she might at most let him feel her up a bit, maybe. Not now, she was going to fuck him. "I fuckin' love your cock Noah."

"Prove it sis."

Holly ran her tongue the along the length of his cock, swirled it around the tip as she felt his hands at the back of her head, grasping handfuls of her hair. They both needed this; the time for teasing was over. She parted her lips and took her brother into her mouth.

"Ohhhh," Noah groaned.

She pulled his cock out with a soft pop. You like?" Before he could answer the question she engulfed his cock again, quickly finding her rhythm of sucking, licking and kissing his shaft, head, and balls, her hands grasping his hips as she worked him.

"Fuckin' hell Holly ... that's good."

Holly didn't hear his praise; she was lost in her lust. All she knew or cared about was the cock before her. It was hard and thick with veins that ran along the shaft, and it was Noah's. The thought of having her brother in her mouth was driving her wild. The thought of her fiancé stuck at work while she cheated on him with her brother drove her crazy with lust. The whole scene was wrong on so many levels and she loved it. "My brother's cock ... my brother ... my mouth," she began to chant as she kissed and licked his shaft.

"Oh fuuuck Holly, I can't take much more."

"Cum baby, do it," she moaned as she returned his cock to the heat of her mouth.

"Where?"

"Mffph," she replied not taking his cock form her mouth, her hands now joining in the fun, stroking his saliva soaked shaft as she sucked.

"Holly," he grunted.

She felt his grip on her head tighten as his cock began to pulse filling her mouth with his cum. All the thoughts running through her head combined with knowing her brother was cumming in her mouth sent her over the edge. She groaned as an orgasm rippled though her body while she struggled to swallow his cum. Noah's groaning and twitching slowed as she felt his cum leak out past her lips. She held his cum in her mouth as she slid his cock from her mouth. Noah was looking down at her when she looked up, grinning. She opened her mouth showing him the mouthful of his cum she had collected, small trails of it running along her cheeks and chin.

"Fuckin' hell that's hot," he groaned.

Holly tossed her head back and swallowed with an exaggerated gulp, making a production out of it. Her time in drama class well spent she thought. As she returned her gaze to him he lunged at her, "Ahhh." She squealed as Noah suddenly dropped to his knees, grabbing her about the hips, pulling her ass in one quick movement to the edge of the bed. The forgotten shorts and panties tangled about her ankles stopping his planned assault.

"Damnit," he muttered.

"Poor Noah, no sister pussy for him."

"Like hell," he said as he untangled her feet, sending her shoes, shorts, and panties flying one by one around the room.

"Oh Noah," she sighed as he freed her legs, pushing them apart. She looked down between her spread legs at her brother as he worked himself free of his own clothing.

"Bra off, if you please," he said to her as he saw her watching him.

"Yes sir baby brother," she replied, quickly removing her bra, tossing it behind her. She watched as her now fully naked brother, his recently spent cock, still glistening with her saliva came toward her. "Oohhh," she groaned when she felt their skin come together as he laid his body down on top of hers. She wrapped her legs around his waist as they began to kiss, her hands stroking his back.

"You taste good sis."

"Yeah I bet, I'm all sweat ... it's so hot in here."

"I love it."

"Yeah?"

"Yep, love it so much I'm gonna lick your body till I reach that little pink pussy of yours."

"Please do," she groaned as he began moving down her body stopping to pay attention to her firm tits. "Oohh fuck Noah, suck em ... suck em." He continued down her body licking around her navel as she ran her fingers in his hair, pushing him lower. "Oh god Noah, eat me ... please."

"I dunno."

"Please," she whined pursing her lips into a pout.

"Your pussy is perfect Holly."

"Shut up." She felt him push her legs apart as he began to kiss and lick her belly and thighs. "Fuck Noah, eat me already," she moaned, rotating her hips.

"Payback sis ... payback."

"Fucker," Holly smiled. "Ooooh fuuck," she yelled out as his mouth closed around her clit. "Oh oh Noah ... ooh god." She squirmed on the bed, grinding her mound against his face. "Gonna ... gonna ... oooh so good," she shuddered as he continued to bathe her pussy in the heat of his mouth, the friction of her gyrations, his tongue on her clit. Then she felt his fingers go to work. Her mind reeled again as she thought about whose fingers were inside her. Her brother had his face between her spread legs as he worked his fingers inside her body. It was so wrong ... so very wrong. "Oh fuck!" She yelled out as her orgasm hit her, waves of pleasure as she clamped her legs to her brother's head.

"Damn sis, someone is going to call the cops with you shrieking like that."

Holly laid back on the bed, breathing heavy with her legs over the bed's edge, spread apart. She was dripping with sweat. The room felt sauna hot. Her mind wandered as she lay there, she thought about their childhood, growing up, fighting all the time. She thought about the taboo of it all, how everyone she knew would freak out about it. She wondered if anyone she knew was doing something similar, if she was it couldn't be all that uncommon. She thought about Jack, still at work while she was having so much illicit fun.

"Holy fuck Noah," she said as Noah got up to get some water.

"Yeah," he panted, "incredible."

"I can't believe this but ... I fucking love your dick."

"Oh shit Holly."

"Seriously bro, I love dicks and I love sucking a nice hard cock ... I've never had one as hard as yours was."

"I've never been so hard ... it's all because of you Holly."

Holly sat up, resting back on her elbows as she watched Noah disappear into the small bathroom. "Hey Noah, you know how I was saying I can't guarantee how far I might be able to go with this whole incest thing?"

"Yeah."

"I know how far now."

"And?" He asked as the sounds of running water stopped.

"All the fucking way Noah ... all the way."

"Really?"

"Yeah, I want to fuck you ... I want to ride my baby brother's cock until he explodes in my pussy."

"Hottest thing I've ever heard," he said as he walked back into the main room.

"Bring that big dick of yours over here will ya?"

Holly watched as Noah walked toward her bed, standing where he had been when she had blown him moments before, "geez Noah it's hard again already."

"My sister is hot; she makes it do that when she's around."

"Oh my, is this really for me?" she reached out wrapping her hand around his shaft, "oh my god Noah, I wish I had known you wanted me sooner."

"Meaning what?"

"Meaning we could have been fucking like bunnies years ago."

"That would have been epic."

"Indeed ... all those summer days I wasted out by the pool tanning when I could have been on your cock riding it to heaven."

"My sister has a dirty mouth."

She looked up at him, her hand stroking his cock, "only when my brother is pumping his jizz into it."

"Goddamn Holly."

She snickered, "anyway ... this dick is all hard and tasty looking." Holly leaned forward running her tongue along his length, "but my pussy is wet and empty. I'd really like my brother to shove his cock into it. How about it bro ... will ya pin me to the bed with your big hard dick and fuck me silly?"

"Waited all my life to hear that," he said pushing her onto her back, "I'm gonna fuck your brains out."

Holly spread her legs as wide as she could as Noah climbed onto the bed, moving between her outstretched legs. She watched intently as her brother knelt on the bed, his cock in hand. He leaned forward pressing the tip against her opening, "ooh god ... my brother is gonna put his big hard cock in me. Look at me Noah, this is our moment ... watch me as you fill me." She looked at him, watching intently as he pushed forward ... both siblings lost in lust as they studied the others expression as they joined for the first time. Her eyes rolled back as he pushed forward, she felt the pressure of his cock moving inside her, stretching her. "Oooooh shit, shit ... it's slidin ..." her voice trailed off as she felt him continue to fill her, "so good Noah ... so fucking good," she dropped onto her back with her brother on top of her, their sweaty bodies together, her legs wrapped around waist, his cock filling her.

"You feel so good Holly," he whispered in her ear.

"So do you Noah ... best dick ever."

After a few moments, Noah began to move, rocking his hips, slowly thrusting in and out of his sister. Gradually their thrusting picked up speed, his hips rocking as she writhed under him, her hands on his ass as she desperately tried to take every inch of him into her.

"Fuck me Noah ... fuck your big sister ... give it to her."

"You wanna fuck?"

"God yes ... please fuck me bro ... fuck me," her legs tightened around his waist as his ass bobbed up and down, his cock sliding in and out of her. She smiled as she noticed the steady squeaking the motel mattress made as Noah thrust into her. The room was filled with the sounds of straining bed springs, the wet slapping of bodies and their gasping breaths. She was surprised by how unbelievably erotic it all was, how turned on she was, how she never wanted to stop.

"You feel so good Holly."

"You like my pussy baby?"

"So fuckin' good sis."

"I love your cock Noah, love it too much," she tightened her grip on his ass. "You're gonna make me cum if you keep this up."

"Fuck yes," he sped up his thrusting spurred on by her moaning.

"Ohh, god ... oh god ... I'm gonna ... gonna ... " her words cut off as her body began to spasm, her legs clamped around her brother's waist, her finger nails digging into the flesh of his ass. "Ugghh," she moaned as waves of orgasmic bliss washed over her.

"Having fun?" Noah asked as her spasms slowed.

Holly looked up at her brother as he continued to slowly move in and out of her. "So good ... do me doggy now stud?"

"My pleasure," he replied moving away from her, his cock slipping out.

Holly quickly rolled over; placing her head on the mattress as she raised her ass in the air, exposing her well fucked pussy to her brother. "Stick it back in baby ... please," she whined while looking over her shoulder at him.

Noah looked at his sister, her ass in the air, her pink pussy exposed, her body glistening with sweat, "whatever my sister wants."

"Oh really?" She cooed as his cock entered her again. "If only I had known it was this easy to get my way with you."

He grabbed handfuls of her tight ass and began pumping into her, "tightest ... pussy ....ever."

"Your ... cock is ... so fucking ... big," she grunted as the sounds of the squeaky mattress and wet slapping sounds filled the room again.

"Rise up Holly."

She pushed up on her hands as Noah continued his assault on her, as she began to look over her shoulder at him, he grabbed a handful of her hair, pulling her head back, "oh fuck Noah."

"Take it sis," he grunted through clenched teeth as he began to slide into her as fast as he could, holding a handful of her blonde curls in one hand and gripping her ass with the other.

"Uuuggh ... my god Noah ... fuck ... fuck ... you're so good ... I fucking love fucking you."

"Who?"

"You I love fucking you."

Leaning forward he slowed their pace as he whispered into her ear, "and who am I Holly?"

"My brother ... my really big little brother."

"You like fucking your brother?"

"God yes ... so much ... too much ... I love his dick."

"Uuggh," he grunted as their bodies slapped against each other, "gotta stop soon."

"No," she nearly yelled in a panic as she reached back for him, "don't stop ... I'm close ... give it to me."

"Gonna lose it."

"Just go ... fill me ... I want your cum ... fill me baby brother." She felt his hand clamp down on her as his cock began to pulse inside of her. He stayed deep inside her, pulling her hair as she felt his hot cum filling her. Her brother was cumming inside of her. Little Noah, her annoying baby brother had his cock buried to the hilt in her pussy and was now filling her with his cum. It was too much for her. Another orgasm hit as Noah's cock pulsed in her pussy. "OH MY GOD!"

Noah released his grip on her hair, her head drooped forward as her held onto her ass, massaging her sweaty cheeks as he held her tight to him.

"Oh my god Noah ... you're a beast ... my poor little pussy."

"That was the hottest thing I've ever done Holly ... that I'll ever do," he said as he looked down at his sister's back, wet with sweat, her head resting on the mattress.

"Glad you liked it bro," she said as he released his grip on her ass. She fell forward onto her belly, his softening cock slipped out of her. She lay still as Noah climbed onto the bed next to her, looking up at the ceiling.

"I loved it Holly."

"Me too ... god help me but I love incest."

"Hot isn't it."

"Fuck yes it is. I was worried trying this might fuck us up, but now I just need to figure out how we can do it again."

"You want to do it again?"

"Hell yes ... a lot ... we have a lot of time to make up for Noah dear."

"I'll jump in that pussy anytime sis."

She looked over at him, "umm, thanks I suppose."

The quiet chatting of the siblings was interrupted by her phone. The alarm she had set was going off. Their window of opportunity was closing. "I don't want to go Noah, I came in here unsure about so much and now I don't want to ever leave."

"This was the best afternoon ever sis. Thanks for being so open minded about it all, it means everything to me ... really."

She reached over to him running her hand across his chest, "thank you bro ... I feel really good right now and not just because of the orgasms. I feel loved more than I ever have."

"What do we do now?"

"Well, we go home and dream about today and then we meet up and align our schedules," she said with a smile as she stood up looking around the room for her clothes.

"Yeah?"

"Oh yeah," she said as she leaned over to him. "I do have one more condition."

"And that is?"

"In addition to the, no one ever can know rule ... you also have to promise to be my fuck buddy from now on."

"Deal."

"Now get off your ass and help me find my clothes, you threw them all over the room."

MILFs Do It Better (Milfs)

Mother and son cannot hide their attraction any longer

Erin was washing the dishes when her stepson came into the kitchen from the pool. He took out a bag of chips from the pantry and stuffed a handful in his mouth.

"What's for dinner tonight?" Dominic said.

Erin turned around and without thinking checked him out from head to toe. Dominic was wearing short swimming trunks that clung to his body like a band-aid. His skin was glistening from the pool water and sweat. Erin let her eyes trail over his muscular arms, his sculpted chest, bulging abs and lower, following with her eyes the muscles that led to his crotch. She let her eyes rest on Dominic's swimming trunks. She turned back to the dishes when she realized what she was doing.

"Uh...Lasagna," she said.

"I fucking love your lasagna," Dominic said and kissed her on the cheek as he walked past her out of the kitchen. Erin blushed then called out "no cussing!" as she stared at Dominic's ass.

Erin let her hands do the work of washing dishes. It was automatic. Her muscles had their own memory and they took over the task, freeing her mind to do some serious thinking.

Ever since Dominic turned 18 it seemed like he has gotten closer to her. Closer than a stepson should. She always had a good relationship with Dominic. There was a lot of love and warmth between them. But ever since he grew up to be an attractive man, she thought that there was something more behind the hugs and kisses he was always giving her.

She turned red every time that thought popped in her mind. She would shake her head and rub her face with her hands. She'd let her head rest on the palm of her hand and she'd laugh to herself. She put the thought out of her mind, until the next time Dominic did something oddly affectionate. A comment here, a brush there, a hug that was held for too long, a look in the eyes.

She's been with plenty of men in her life. She knew the signs, the subtle cues that men and women give each other. The human mating dance. She thought she was seeing it with Dominic. But he was her stepson so she convinced herself she was misinterpreting it. He was just being affectionate towards his stepmother. Nothing unusual about that.

She was convinced until Dominic gave her another signal. Then another. Then another.

Her stepson was a man in the full sense of the word. He grew up to be tall and handsome, just like his father. He had the lean, muscular built of a teenage athlete. He was the star football player of his high school, due to go to a top college on a football scholarship. He had his father's green eyes. Their intense color was visible from across the room. He styled his light brown hair in a messy manner that made him look adorable. He looked like a younger and more virile version of her husband. And she was massively attracted to her husband. But he was always away on business while she played a stay-at-home mom.

When she thought about it she laughed at the situation. She wasn't surprised, that under these circumstances, she found herself attracted to her stepson. It would be strange if she wasn't. She was 35 years old and still considered herself to be in her peak. She had strong sexual urges, which her husband satisfied thoroughly whenever he was around. The problem was that he wasn't around and there was only so much a vibrator could accomplish. She was horny and stuck in a house with a young version of her husband. She laughed to herself at the thought. There was nothing else she could do. She laughed every time the thought of acting on her desire entered her mind. She swatted it away in her mind. Then she convinced herself again that there was nothing behind Dominic's behavior. She was misinterpreting his affection.

Dominic's swimming trunks were dry. He was wearing a tank top revealing his tan, muscular arms. As Erin served the lasagna, she couldn't help but look over his bulging biceps, and forearms built like steel cords.

She sat across the table from him and ate in silence. She tried not to stare. Dominic was a growing boy and he ate a ton of food. He stuffed his face without pausing to breathe. The only sounds were Dominic's chewing, punctuated by the sounds of his gustatory approval.

Erin kept her eyes on the food. She chased the bits of lasagna around the plate with her fork. Her muscles were doing their own thing again as her mind ran around different thoughts and memories. She thought about the time she came home early from her friend's house and heard Dominic and his girlfriend having sex in his room.

"You're too big," she heard the girl say. She remembered standing outside the door to his room and listening. She remembered feeling dirty. She remembered telling her body to get away, to walk outside, to quit her voyeurism. But her body didn't listen. She stood there, and eavesdropped.

"Let me make you more wet, I'll lick your pussy," she heard her stepson say. His words made her own pussy wetter then, and the memory was making her wet now, as she ate across the table from him. She looked up at him and his eyes met hers. He smiled with a mouthful of lasagna. Erin quickly returned her gaze to the plate.

"What's wrong?" Dominic said, as he wiped his mouth with his hand. Erin looked out the window at the sun setting over the hills in the distance. It has been a very hot day. She wore a very revealing sundress and right now, under Dominic's gaze, she felt naked.

"Nothing is wrong Dominic. How's the food?" she said, trying to change the subject.

Dominic held up an empty plate.

"Amazing as always," he said. He got up from his seat, walked around the table and kissed Erin on the cheek. She closed her eyes as his lips met her warm skin and inhaled sharply. Dominic's natural, masculine musk entered her nostrils, traveled to her lungs, entered her bloodstream, made her dizzy like a drug. Dominic went over to the sink and left his plate there.

"Thank you mom," he said. "I'm going to be in my room."

Erin put the fork down and stared at the setting sun outside. She closed her eyes and leaned her head back. She touched the spot on her cheek where her stepson's lips have been a second ago and opened her eyes. She stared at the ceiling. She ran her other hand down her body, between her legs and touched her pussy over her panties. It was wet.

She chased the pieces of lasagna around her plate without thinking about it. She wasn't hungry anymore. Not for food. She picked up her plate and swept the lasagna into the trash. She put the plate in the sink then leaned against the counter with her arms spread wide. She looked at her reflection in the window. It was a ghostly image, transparent in the shadows. She laughed and shook her head.

Erin was tired. The constant heat has worn her out, and the meal she just ate contributed. She turned off the light in the kitchen and walked upstairs to her bedroom.

She passed Dominic's door and slowed down. She stood there in the silent hallway and listened. She saw a yellow glow coming from under the door and shadows flicking across the strip of light. She turned her body towards the door and leaned against the wall next to it.

She squinted and furrowed her brow. Usually there was music or video game sounds coming from Dominic's room. No matter what he was doing, whether it was homework, reading, or his girlfriend, there was always music. But the hallway was silent. There were no sounds coming from his room. Only flickering shadows beneath the door.

Erin raised her hand to knock on the door but stopped. She let her arm drop at her side. She stood there staring at the door. She put her hand on the door handle and pushed the door quietly open. Through the tiny gap between the door and the doorframe she saw the back of Dominic's head. He was still wearing the same thing. He had headphones covering his ears. The desk lamp on his desk was on. From where Erin was standing, the light was blocked by Dominic's head, making it look like he had a halo around it. Erin stared at that light effect and didn't notice what Dominic was doing.

His head blocked half of the computer screen in front of him. Erin opened the door wider, without thinking, trying to figure out what she was seeing. She squinted and stepped into the room. Then she noticed Dominic's right arm shaking. Her eyes darted back to the screen and Erin saw the naked legs of two people, bouncing rhythmically. She covered her mouth as she realized what Dominic was doing. He was masturbating to porn.

She stood in the middle of Dominic's room covering her hand with her mouth. She didn't realize how far inside the room she has walked. She stepped slightly to the right to get a full view of the screen as her shock turned into curiosity.

Stepson fucking a MILF, was the title above the video. Erin's skin became hot. Her eyes opened wide and her brain spun around in her skull. Her eyes darted to Dominic's hand. The view of his cock was blocked by his muscular arm. Erin leaned against the dresser and extended her neck trying to catch a glimpse of the penis that gave Dominic's girlfriend so much trouble. As she transferred her weight to her hand, it slid from underneath her. She has put it on some lose papers. She stumbled momentarily then caught herself and straightened instantly.

Dominic pulled his swimming trunks up and shot up from his seat. The headphone cable was ripped out from the computer as he did so. The loud moans of a mature pornstar filled the entire house.

"What the fu...Mom!" he yelled out as he covered his crotch with his hands. He turned halfway away from Erin, who stood there, without a word or thought. Only her eyes moved, from Dominic's face, to the computer screen, to his crotch. She has caught him.

Erin regained her composure, but didn't know what to say. She mumbled some half-finished words as she turned around and shuffled out of the room, shutting the door behind her. She heard Dominic fumble with the computer keyboard as she made her exit and the moans coming from the speakers ceased. Erin walked fast to her empty bedroom and closed the door. She pressed her back against the cool wood of the door and put her hand to her forehead, covering her eyes. Her entire face felt on fire. She squeezed her eyes shut. She held her breath. The back of her head hit the door with a thump. Her hand traveled slowly over the folds and wrinkles of her dress. Down over her breasts, her stomach, her thigh. It traveled under her skin, caressing her thigh, her fire-hot skin. Her hand touched her panties. They were soaked.

When Erin went down to the kitchen in the morning she found a used pan in the sink. The smell of bacon hung in the air. Usually she made Dominic's breakfast. This morning he got up earlier than her and made it himself. She felt a tinge of disappointment as she stared at the dirty plate poking out of the sink. Her eyes rested on it but her mind wasn't receiving that input. Her mind was replaying the events of last night. Erin relived all the sounds, sights and feelings so completely that she almost didn't hear the front door slamming shut. She blinked and turned towards the front of the house a few seconds after the sound stopped. She walked to the front door and looked out the window. She saw Dominic jumping on the back of his friend's jeep, which was filled with his friends. He had a towel hung across his back. He was going to the beach. She listened to the car starting up, loud music blasting out of its speakers, the bass shaking the window in front of her face. As the car pulled away from the curb with a screech of the tires she saw Dominic glance back and their eyes met. She quickly stepped behind the curtain and listened to the music receding into silence.

She took few deep breaths when she realized her heart was beating too fast. She laughed to herself as she slouched her shoulders forward and let her arms hang loose in front of her. She straightened up and went to the kitchen to make herself breakfast.

When she was done drinking her coffee and checking news on her tablet, she made a to-do list on a piece of paper. It was laundry day. First thing on the list.

She had to collect the laundry from Dominic's room. She put her hand on the door to his room, but didn't push it open right away. Flashes of last night passed in front of her eyes. She heard the moans coming out of a speaker in her mind.

Stepson fucking a MILF. That was the title of the video that Dominic was watching. She bit her lip as she considered the implications. As her mind worked at a thousand thoughts a second, she unconsciously pressed her hand against the door harder and harder until it snapped open. She saw the black computer monitor with a beam of light across it. It was lit up like a prized artifact sitting in an ancient tomb in an adventure movie. She stepped into the room. The air felt heavy. The heat that already assaulted the earth that morning made her skin slick and shiny with sweat. She was there for the laundry. But she felt like she was trespassing.

She moved her head away from the computer and her eyes followed after. She scanned Dominic's room. It was messy. Unusually messy. Her stepson wasn't the tidiest teenager, but he usually kept things in a better order than they were now.

Erin thought: he didn't clean up last night—he just went to sleep right after what happened to avoid embarrassment. And he didn't clean up this morning—he just wanted to escape being alone in the house with me. He wanted to escape that awkward conversation that was surely to follow. He most likely didn't realize it was just as awkward for me as it was for him.

Erin got the laundry basket out of Dominic's closet and picked up few stray pieces of clothing scattered about the room. She picked up his boxer briefs and quickly threw them into the basket. She didn't want to find cum stains on them. Her eyes opened wide at the thought. She picked up the basket and started to walk out the room when her eyes fell across the computer screen again.

She stood staring at it like it was a riddle she needed to figure out before she could proceed with her life. She cocked her head to the side. She pursed her lips. She breathed slow, deep breaths through her nose. She put the laundry basket down in slow motion. She straightened up the same way. Then she walked over to the computer and sat in Dominic's chair. She looked behind her at the open door to his room. The house was completely quiet. Outside, she could hear only the sound of sprinklers in her neighbor's backyard. She stared at the empty doorway for a long time. Then slowly her head turned back and she stared at her own reflection in the black computer screen. Without input from her brain her hand rose, covered the computer mouse and clicked a button a couple of times. The fans on the computer came on, lights lit up, hard drive made noises. The screen displayed the logo of the college Dominic was going to attend in the fall. There were various files and folder scattered on the desktop. Erin's eyes scanned over them without absorbing any of the names. She double clicked a familiar icon. Internet browser. Then she looked over her shoulder at the empty doorway. She looked back at the screen and adjusted in the chair.

She clicked few times and bit her lip. Displayed on the screen was Dominic's browsing history. Her eyes darted down the long list of names. Adrenaline clawed her stomach from inside. She covered her eyes with both her hands. Then she peeked between her fingers.

Stepson fucking a MILF. That was the name at the top. Her eye moved down a tiny fraction. Hot mom being fucked by a young stud. That was the second entry. Her eye moved down. MILF Hunter – Victoria. Mature woman covered in cum. Milf fucked by two young workers. Brunette Milf does it all. Sexy blonde wife orgasms on his...

The list went on. Then there was a pause. The history displayed normal websites. Forum about motorcycles. Google. Facebook. College website. Then a block of porn websites.

The neighbor's dog started barking and the sound startled Erin. She clicked at the X in the top right corner of the browser and kept clicking. She hit the power button on the computer and it went into sleep mode. Then she saw her face reflected in the black computer monitor. She wasn't frowning. She wasn't crying. Her teeth reflected brightly in the dark monitor. Erin was smiling.

Erin was watching TV when she heard the front door close. The sound was quieter than the usual sound that signaled that Dominic or her husband was back home. She looked over the backrest. Dominic, with a towel over his back, was turning a corner to walk up the stairs. The TV was playing loud enough for him to hear, but he didn't look over. He didn't greet his stepmom. He looked down on the ground and made his way to the stairs as fast as he could.

"Dominic," Erin called out. She made sure to put on a smile. She didn't want Dominic to be scared. Didn't want him to think he was going to receive a stern lecture. She didn't think there was anything wrong with men masturbating.

Dominic stopped on the stairs. She saw him immobile for few seconds, his hand on the railing. His head was covered by a hat, its bill turned back. She saw him look down on the ground then turn around.

He was wearing a blue and white striped tank top, and black swimming trunks. His skin was bronzed from the sun. As he came closer Erin could smell the sunscreen. He came right up to her, behind the couch. He looked down on her with a face that betrayed fear and annoyance. Erin was still sitting on the couch, turned around towards Dominic. Her face was level with Dominic's crotch. She did her best not to let her eyes wander there. She maintained eye contact.

"Yes, mother?" he said. Erin patted a spot on the couch next to her.

"Sit down, I'm not going to bite."

Dominic looked up at the ceiling and grunted. He walked around the couch and sat next to Erin. He held his towel on his lap.

Erin wore a short dress with a very low neckline. Her full, round breasts were squeezed together by the bra she chose to wore. Her skin was glistening with a slight layer of sweat. She put her elbow on the back of the couch and propped her head up with her hand. She leaned over towards Dominic who was sitting with straight back, facing the front of the couch. His eyes rested on the floor. His fingers picked at loose threads of the towel.

Three long seconds of silence passed.

"Mom, I don't want to talk about it," Dominic said. He couldn't take the silence. Erin was smiling. Dominic turned towards her and his eyes instantly darted to Erin's cleavage. His face started to take on a panicked expression, then reset as his eyes shot back up to meet hers. Erin saw Dominic's pupils dilate.

"It's okay Dominic, it's nothing to be ashamed about. It's natural. It's not like I didn't know you've been doing it."

Dominic turned away and stared straight ahead.

"Okay, then we don't need to talk about it, right?"

Erin tilted her head to get a better look at Dominic's face.

"How's Jessica?" Erin said.

"She's good."

"Are you guys going to stay together once you go to college?"

Dominic's posture relaxed. His shoulders moved down an inch and he smoothed the towel with his palms. Then he looked at his stepmom. His eyes once again did a jump, from her breasts to her eyes. Click, click.

"Um...If you asked me that a few months ago I would say yes, but...I don't know now. She's too immature."

Erin nodded and smiled. She straightened her arm and laid it across the backrest. Her hand was behind Dominic's head.

"So you want someone mature?" Erin said. Dominic nodded. She could see his pupils growing larger. She looked down at his lap.

"This towel is so sandy," she said. "Let me put it in the laundry."

She grabbed the towel and pulled it. Dominic held it in place with his strong arms.

Andrea's Guinea Pig (BDSM)

Unsuspecting man is drawn into the BDSM scene.

My name is John and I suppose I've lived a fairly quiet life, a few wild experiences when I was young but nothing too exciting ever happens to me nowadays, until recently that is. I'm in my late 50's and moved to the valley three years ago with my wife Rosa, an attractive lady in her early 50's standing at 5 feet 2 inches with big tits 40D they were the first thing I ever noticed about her. Trouble is in recent years she has lost all interest in sex, always has a good excuse to say no and has let herself go a bit, putting on a bit of weight and letting her belly get a bit flabby. I sometimes think she let herself go deliberately to make herself less attractive. The kids had grown up and settled down and I thought we were set up for a quiet rural retirement.

It wasn't long after we moved that it became clear that Rosa had developed an intense dislike for our next door neighbour Andrea, I had seen Rosa take similar dislikes in the past, normally the target of her hatred was an attractive woman with a reputation for liking other women's husbands and it has to be said Andrea has a body most women half her age would die for. She is late 40's and has a very tight body which looks great in her riding outfit, skin-tight jodhpurs and close fitting white shirt. She is about 5 feet 3 inches and around 8 stones her legs and ass are perfectly formed and clearly displayed in her jodhpurs and I would guess her tits measure in at around 36C and always look to stand very proud.

Once I noticed Rosa's dislike for Andrea I decided it may be entertaining to keep an eye on what was happening and whenever we went to the local pub I would discretely listen in to the local ladies gossiping, talk about catty! Andrea was always the main topic of conversation, it transpired that she had always been single but never went short of some male company and the women of the valley were all frightened she would tempt their husbands. It appeared Andrea worked for herself as she was often around during the day and as I work shifts I often saw her and we would speak politely but never got into deep conversation.

This went on for about 2 years and it looked as though our quiet life was here to stay, Rosa annoyed me with her constant bitchy comments about out neighbour and I started to challenge her, asking what she had done to deserve such animosity, Rosa's response was always to say she has affairs with married men but didn't know the names of any. One day I was so sick of hearing these comments I told her I thought it was time she backed off, she had no evidence to support her allegations, only the valley gossip. She turned angrily and asked why I was defending her and asked if I was having an affair with her, this developed into a full blown row and ended with me storming out, slamming the door and going to the pub where I definitely had too much to drink. I got home late and Rosa was asleep, rather than risk another row by waking her I went in the spare room.

I woke next morning with a stinking hangover, my first in years which probably made it seam worse, Rosa had gone to work and I had a day off so I grabbed a coffee and sat in the garden hoping a little fresh air would help. I had not been there long when Andrea peaked over the fence and asked if I was OK, I said "what do you mean?" she said she heard the row last night and thought I looked a bit rough. I said "I feel rough, I have a stinking hangover." Andrea said she had a good hangover cure and invited me in for a sample. I thanked her and went into her house for the first time, it was very modern, bright and airy, she looked stunning in a mini skirt that would certainly have upset the local ladies, and a tight fitting shirt that made it obvious she was not wearing a bra, and it was obvious she didn't need one.

Andrea brought me an ice cold shot glass filled with some dark liquid, I asked "what is it?" "Jagermeister" she answered "it's a great hangover cure, just knock it back." I drank it and Andrea made coffee, we sat and chatted for some time. After about 20 minutes I started to feel much better I was fascinated to discover that she was a designer of furniture and visited peoples homes to design bespoke items which she the commissioned from a local craftsman. In her spare time she liked to ride and had her own stallion stabled nearby. I asked if I could see some of her designs and she happily brought out some of her design books, the furniture was all ultra modern, clean lines and bright colours, she told me that all the furniture in her own home was of her own design. I was lazily thumbing through the designs when I came across what looked like a coffin she saw the shocked look on my face and looked at the page, "oh! I didn't realise that was in there that's part of a special order I'm working on" she said. I asked her who would have her design a coffin she told me she had recently met some people who were planning to open a BDSM club in the nearby town and they asked her if she could design some special furniture and equipment to fit the place out.

She said it was actually quite good fun to think that her furniture could be used to restrain people and all in the pursuit of pleasure, she said the biggest problem was she couldn't get her usual craftsman to make the equipment as he was married to a local minister and would not approve so she was going to have a go at making it herself. She told me she had done a lot of construction when she was at college, she has a gym in the basement and keeps very fit so was confident she could cope. We chatted a while longer and she showed me the gym and invited me to come over for a workout any-time.

A few days later I saw Andrea again and she said she had started constructing the equipment for the club and asked if I could give her a helping hand, I went with her and she took me into the workshop she had created in the unused part of the basement. Standing against one wall was a padded X shaped cross with a hole in the end of each spar, she said she had never designed anything like this before and wanted to make sure it worked. I asked what she wanted me to do, she said "stand against the cross and let me tie you to it" I must have looked worried as she quickly said "don't worry I'm not going to torture you". With some trepidation I stood with my back to the cross and she pulled down two padded leather bracelets that fastened easily around my wrists with Velcro, the bracelets were attached to ropes which went through holes at the top of the cross. She then fastened similar attachments to my ankles and pulled the ropes through pulling my legs uncomfortably apart, I tried to resist without success, then my arms were similarly stretched.

I was spread-eagled and unable to move, Andrea had a broad smile on her face "can you move" she asked.

"That's a stupid question" I retorted "how did you manage to do this so easily, I was trying to resist."

"I know, my contraption really works doesn't it"

"How did you do it?"

"A simple system of pulleys and I used a rock climbing aide to lock the rope automatically, do you think the club members will like it?"

"How would I know? I've never been in such a place and why would anyone want to be secured like this?"

"Well, just think of what I could do to you now, I could do anything I wanted" she said whilst moving her perfect body against me, "what would you like me to do?"

"I don't want you to do anything to me I'm married."

"OK I'll believe you" she laughed "are the cuffs painful?"

"No"

"Is the cross comfortable against your back?"

"That's not how I would describe it, I'm bloody uncomfortable, my arms and legs are stretched to their limits."

"But is it painful?"

"Not quite."

"Great, that's exactly what I wanted."

"So when are you going to release me?"

"When you ask nicely."

"OK, please let me down Andrea."

Then with four quick movements the ropes came lose and Andrea swiftly released the Velcro fastenings and I was free in seconds. She looked very pleased with herself and asked me to stay for coffee, I said I could do with something stronger after that experience, "whisky?" she asked "that will do nicely" I said.

We than sat and talked over a couple of drinks whilst she interrogated me about my experience on the cross. She was obviously delighted with the success of her design and it's efficiency and then said she needed to run one more test before she could take it to the club, she needed to try it on someone naked so she could ensure there was no chaffing.

"No way I said standing to leave."

"Oh, go on, be a sport."

"No way."

"How about just bearing you wrists and ankles?" she said "so I can ensure the cuffs are OK, I promise not to pull them too tight."

Reluctantly I agreed, removed my shoes and socks and rolled my shirtsleeves up.

"Stand facing the cross" she said "I want to make sure it works both ways."

Once again the four cuffs were attached to me and the ropes quickly pulled through until I was stretched to my limit. Again Andrea stood very close to me and spoke quietly into my ear "do the cuffs hurt?"

"No" I said "but I'm bloody uncomfortable"

"Your supposed to be" stroking my stretched ass cheeks she whispered "anything you fancy me doing?"

"Let me go"

"OK" she said and released me as easily as before. "Thanks for your help and sorry if you felt threatened but I had to know my design works, once my clients see this I hope I will get the contract for the rest of the kit, it should be worth a tidy sum."

"Good luck" I said as I left trying to hide a raging hard-on.

I spent the next few days struggling to get my session with Andrea out of my mind and kept imagining myself naked, being tied up by her as she tormented me with her perfect body. It had been years since I'd had so many hard ons or wanked so much.

About a week later, just as I was starting to get these thoughts out of my mind she knocked the door and asked if I could help her test some more equipment, she said she could trust me not to tell others what she was doing and didn't want to involve anyone else. Despite my reservations I agreed and went with her to her workshop, in the middle of the floor was a padded contraption on two levels, I asked "what is that?" "a bondage stool" she said "go kneel on it."

Reluctantly I knelt on the lower level, she told me to lay over the top and fastened a strap across my back then two around my thighs, she pulled out two supports and secured me just below the knees and at the ankles. She then secured my arms and asked my to try to move, I was trapped, the only thing I could move was my head. I watched her move around the room like a predator circling her prey, I watched open mouthed as she removed her jacket revealing her skin-tight white shirt with enough buttons undone to show a wonderful cleavage. She crouched down in front of me, her magnificent tits just inches from my face and whispered "see anything you want? Shame you're all tied up and unable to touch, I bet you have a hard-on" she laughed. "Good, that works well" she said as she quickly released me, "fancy a scotch."

!I think I need one" I said.

We went to the lounge and chatted as we drank her whisky, I was beginning to feel very comfortable in her presence until she brought up Rosa and asked what she would think of me helping her experiments.

"Please don't tell her, she wouldn't understand."

"Don't worry, I know that most of the women around here think I want to fuck their husbands. How wrong they are but why should I worry, I get my kicks from my work, keeping fit and riding my wonderful stallion, I love the lustful looks I get from those useless wankers and the looks of envy from their inadequate wives. I find it quite a laugh."

For the next few weeks I had regular visits from Andrea asking me to test equipment with her, some were more unpleasant than others but all were extremely well made and appeared to be very safe, I was becoming more and more comfortable in Andrea's company and found myself fantasizing about bondage and being dominated by a beautiful woman. I was regularly secured to various devices and she always teased me and I always ended up with a rampant hard-on but she never exposed more than some cleavage she never touched my genitals, though she went very close at times.

Last week my wife had to go away overnight on business, so I took an early shower, slipped on a pair of shorts and a towelling robe and settled down with a beer to watch TV. Andrea chose that evening to ask for my help again. She came around in her riding gear, skin-tight jodhpurs, white shirt and long hacking jacket. She said she had invented an exciting new device and was eager to try it out, I said I would get dressed and follow in a few minutes. She said she needed to test this item with me naked, I said "No way" she said I could keep my shorts on but it would not be possible to do the tests with me fully dressed. It took her about 10 minutes to persuade me but eventually I agreed and followed her to her workshop. What I saw surprised me, it looked like a padded cross (Christian shaped), parallel to the floor on a wide metal frame. The "vertical" was about 6 inches wide with a circular extension on the top and the cross piece about 3 inches wide, there were various leather straps hanging below.

I was feeling very apprehensive as Andrea invited me to remove my robe and slippers and lay on the cross resting my head in the padded circle, she asked me again if I was prepared to go naked, I said "no".

"OK, no problem" she said laughing and started to secure me to the cross. First she brought padded leather straps up and fastened them around my chest and waist with her usual quick release Velcro fastenings, then she secured my arms in a similar way around top, elbows and wrists so my arms were at right angles to my torso and my hands palm up. She then pulled a lever and the "bottom end" split so that she could secure my legs, two straps on my thighs one below the knees and on around the ankles.

She then stood back to admire her handiwork, you see why I needed you without clothes, I couldn't judge the effectiveness of the straps if there was clothing in the way. She then moved forward and put a strap across my forehead securing my head. I started to get a bit worried as I had never been so immobilized before. I got much more worried when she went to my feet and appeared to press a lever under the cross and I felt my legs being pulled uncomfortably wide apart as the cross was obviously hinged in some way.

She now stepped in between my legs she looked down at me and smiled, "Try to move" she said. I struggled to move but could only move my hands and feet, I tried to rock from side to side, but it was no good, it was obvious she had thought of everything, the device was completely solid, it didn't move even a fraction and the bindings had me completely immobile. "OK" I said "you have excelled yourself with this, I can't move a muscle so now you can let me go".

"Not so quick, I have a lot more experiences lined up for you tonight, don't you think it's getting warm in here" she said as she removed her jacket, I couldn't believe what I saw, her shirt was shaped under her tits which were supported by a quarter cup bra. Her magnificent breasts stood proud and her nipples looked huge and both had rings in them, I'd never seen anyone with pierced nipples before. My cock sprang to attention at this wonderful sight, she produced a sharp knife and swiftly cut down both sides of my shorts then pulled them away leaving totally naked with my cock standing to attention. "He looks nice" she said whilst gently stroking my cock, "I think I will have some fun with him tonight."

"I said I wasn't going naked" I said.

"Too late now" she said "I'm in charge now and you will do with you as I wish".

The next thing I was aware of was something warm and wet on my cock and balls, Andrea was lathering me up for shaving and now produced a cut-throat razor, I fought desperately to escape but there was no chance, she told me it would be safer to keep completely still and started to shave me. My cock rapidly started to droop as this gorgeous woman used this lethal looking weapon. She carefully removed all the hair above then grabbed my balls to stretch the skin for shaving. Suddenly my cock felt very warm as she took me into her mouth to get me erect again so she could effectively remove all my pubic hair. Once she was satisfied that I was completely bald she slapped a hot wet towel on the remove all traces of shaving soap.

"That looks better" she said "I like my men clean shaven"

"I'm not your man" I said

"You are whatever I say you are" she said and slapped a load of ice on my cock. I cried out in pain at this she said "don't worry, I need you flaccid for a while" My cock shrank rapidly then she put a leather strap around the base of my cock and then brought it around my balls with a small strap splitting my balls and took me back into her mouth to make me hard again. This time my erection was painful, the leather was tightening around my cock and balls and my cock was beginning to feel as though it would explode, "that's better" she said.

"Better for who?" I asked

Time to shut you up she said and walked around to my head. She straddled my face and I saw her jodhpurs were completely open at the crotch and her clean shaven pussy was in full view. "Put your tongue out" she said "I need some attention and you'd better be a good pussy eater" and immediately lowered herself onto my face. She worked her pussy into my face, her juices were flowing and tasted sweet, I had a wonderful view of her tits as she looked me directly in the eyes. "Have you ever eaten pussy before" she asked. Unable to answer I tried to shake my head, she smiled and said "well whether you have or not it doesn't matter, you are going to learn to be good."

I was beginning to struggle to breath but she appeared to know just when to stand up and let me breathe, she moved back to my throbbing cock and gently stroked it then produced her riding crop. Smiling she waved the crop in front of my face turned around and I cried out as I felt a sharp pain in my groin, she struck each of my taught balls with a vicious blow.

"I think you're ready now" she said and immediately straddled my pelvis and lowered herself onto my throbbing cock taking me in to the hilt in one steady movement. She then started to slowly rock back and forth, riding my cock as she fondled her own tits and asked me if I would like to lick them. Before I could answer she took hold of the rings in her nipples and pulled them gently, she said "do you like my nipple rings" I said I thought they looked nice. "I'm so pleased" she said "because next time I see you I'm going to have yours done, they're so useful for restraining slaves."

"What makes you think I will let you and I'm not a slave" I said.

"That's exactly what you are and by the time I'm finished with you tonight you will agree to anything I say. You are my slave and you will do whatever I want, or you will learn what pain means." With this she sat up and reached round with both hands taking my balls between her thumbs and fingers, she looked me in the eyes and suddenly squeezed hard, and I mean hard. The pain was intense and I felt my eyes would explode, I begged her to stop she just looked me in the eye and said "are you my slave?"

"Yes" I cried and she released my balls. "Never forget that" she said and started to pinch my nipples with her finger nails "it will be so nice to have these pierced, I could have so much fun with them."

She then started to move a little quicker on my cock, "nearly time for you to cum" she said and speeded up again "this is going to be such a treat for you and a great initiation before you come to the club."

"What makes you think I want to go to that club?" I asked.

"Well, you have been my guinea pig during the development of my equipment so it will only be fair for me to use you as my slave on my opening night next week, you will have such a good time with all the members being able to use you as they wish."

"What do you mean YOUR opening night?"

"Sorry about that little deception, the club is mine, I have always been a dominatrix and have wanted my own club for a long time and now I have a partner I have been able to fulfil my ambition. My partner will be coming round a little later so you can meet her, I'm sure you're going to absolutely love her."

"I won't be able to meet her, you need to let me go before Rosa gets home" I said.

"No you don't, I saw her drive off with a suitcase earlier so I know she's away for the night"

My heart sank, this beautiful woman had me exactly where she wanted me and I was helpless. She started to move quickly and put her hands back on my balls, gently massaging them to make me cum. I could feel my orgasm coming for what seamed an eternity before I exploded, my cock was pulsing wildly and my balls felt as though they were being pulled back into me.

When I finally stopped cumming Andrea smiled and said "I love a man who gives me plenty of spunk, especially when he's going to eat it. Open your mouth wide now so you can clean me out."

"No way" I said and immediately felt my balls being squeezed again.

"You want more of this?" she smiled "open your mouth now or I will squeeze harder"

I had no choice I opened my mouth and she carefully got off my cock slipping her hand over her pussy to hold my spunk in place. She straddled my head facing my feet and lowered herself over my open mouth slipping her hand away at the last moment. For the first time in my life I tasted spunk, it was a bit peppery but not as bad as I feared "use your tongue to clean me" she said.

I felt totally degraded being forced to eat my own cum then I felt her tits resting on my belly and she started to fondle my cock again. "When was the last time you came twice in one night I wonder" she said and I the felt my cock slipping into her mouth. She started to suck vigorously and it was obvious she meant to have me cum again, she let my cock go for a moment and told me to work on her clit, she said if I came before she did she would crush my balls. I started licking around where I though I should and she took me back in her mouth. I began to feel confident that I was doing well when I heard her moaning and felt a vibration on my cock as if she was humming, to my amazement I started to feel the beginnings of another orgasm.

Suddenly I felt someone touching my right hand, this couldn't be Andrea, she was holding my balls, there was someone else in the room. My heart started pounding, I tried to speak but all I could do was grunt, "don't stop licking" said Andrea and went back to work on my cock.

The newcomer gently moulded my hand so that my first two fingers were sticking up, then I felt something warm wrapping around them, my fingers were being swallowed by a shaven pussy, my thumb was pulled into place at the front and a strangely familiar voice said "use those fingers and thumb and make me cum". I was certain I knew the voice but couldn't place it, this made me even more nervous. Then Andrea started to cum, she was rubbing her pussy vigorously on my face, her sweet juices were flooding my mouth and her humming on my cock was bringing me to the brink again. Just when I thought I could hold out no longer she popped the studs on the leather cock harness and I exploded into her mouth, She continued to suck for a short while to make sure I was drained then stood up and went round to the other woman, she kissed her deeply, then I saw their tongues sharing my spunk. I couldn't believe what I was seeing, it was Rosa, my own wife, kissing another woman and sharing my spunk. My previously very conservative wife was dressed in a black lace-up, quarter cup bask with black stocking and suspenders. Her 40D tits looked amazing and she looked much trimmer than I remembered.

"What the hell is going on here" I shouted

"Have you met my new business partner" Andrea asked "I told you that you would love her, What do you think?"

"That's my wife" I said "she doesn't like sex. She hasn't let me touch her in over a year, what have you done to her? She hates you"

"Would you like to tell him Mistress Rosa?"

"I would be delighted Mistress Andrea" said Rosa, "You will notice that Andrea called me mistress and that is what you will call me in future whenever there are no outsiders with us, you will also call Andrea Mistress. Is that clear?"

"Yes" I said and felt Andreas riding crop strike my balls "Yes Mistress" said Andrea,

"OK" I said and felt another painful blow on my balls "OK Mistress" said Rosa "I told you he's a slow learner"

"OK Mistress" I said

"That's better" said Rosa. "You remember the night you picked a fight with me and stormed out to the pub?"

"I didn't pick a fight with you, you were being unreasonable" I said and immediately regretted it as Andrea again used her crop on my abused balls "Never argue with your Mistress" she said.

Rosa continued "well when you slammed the door and went out Mistress Andrea came round to see if I was OK. She had heard you shouting at me, heard the door slam and seen you walking away. I was a bit taken aback at first as I didn't trust her after what the other women had told me but she seamed genuinely concerned about me so I invited her in. I opened a bottle of wine and we chatted, I told her what I had been told about her and she told me she had never had an affair with any of the local men as she was more into the BDSM scene as a dominatrix and would rather whip them than fuck them. I found this both amusing and embarrassing. Mistress Andrea noticed my embarrassment and asked me if I knew anything about BDSM, I said no. And you slave have stopped pleasuring me, move your fingers NOW."

I felt another sharp blow on my balls and heard Andreas voice "Never stop pleasuring your mistress until she gives you permission".

"Thank you Mistress Andrea" said Rosa "I told Mistress Andrea that I knew absolutely nothing about BDSM and had never met anyone who did. She told me she thought I would like it and started to tell me a little, she said she had some DVD's if I fancied seeing some. We took our wine to her place and watched some BDSM scenes, I found myself more turned on than I could ever remember and told her so. We talked about what fun it would be to use you as a slave and I was getting randier and randier. Mistress Andrea asked me when I last had sex and I told her I couldn't remember so she offered to let me use her fucking machine, I must admit I took some convincing but once she got me in position and started the machine I was hooked, before I could cum she stopped the machine, and told me she had a surprise for me, she tied me down saying I would enjoy it more if I felt I couldn't resist and then changed the dildo from a 6" white one to a 10" black one. I pleaded with her to let me go because I thought it would tear me apart but she ignored my pleas and set the machine to work. It was a little painful at first but once my pussy adjusted I loved it and started to fuck back at the machine, Mistress Andrea slowly increased the speed and depth until I was taking the lot and screaming for more. I came more time that night than I had in 10 years and enjoyed Mistress Andrea kissing me as I came over and over again.

"Mistress Andrea told me about her dream of opening a BDSM Club and told me she had premises in mind but she needed a partner to share the costs and work alongside her as a mistress. I was hooked and said I wanted in, despite my lack of experience we decided there and then to go ahead and I told her you would feel bad the next morning after a night at the pub and would be a great guinea pig if she could somehow tempt you. She said that wouldn't be a problem and it appears she was right, she told me after your first session that you were a born slave and knew you were hooked when she noticed your hard-on the first time she tied you to the cross"

"Since then Mistress Andrea has kept me informed about your progress and I have trained regularly with her in her gym. Do you like my new trimmer body?" she said stroking her hands up from her hips until she cupped her breasts.

"Yes" I said "Yes Mistress" but just too late as Andrea had already hit my balls again with the riding crop.

Rosa started to cum on my fingers, "keep that thumb moving" she screamed as she pulled her nipples and rocked violently back and forth covering my hand in her juices as Andrea again kissed her passionately. As she calmed down she said "the look on your face when Mistress Andrea hits your balls really turns me on, I wish I had known the pleasure of pain years ago, and kissing another woman really turns me on as well." She reached down and gently fondled my balls saying "are these hurting you my sweet?"

"Yes Mistress" I answered

She suddenly painfully squeezed my balls "serves you right, YOU should have been giving me the sort of pleasure I've had this past few weeks." Releasing my balls she smiled sweetly and said "Now, where was I?"

I said "you and Mistress Andrea have been training together"

"Mistress" said Andrea as she hit my balls harder than ever.

"Yes I have been working out, getting fit and trim, I have a flat belly again for the first time in years. I have had total body waxing, not a hair on my body, except my head and I'm having my nipples pierced tomorrow" she said as she tweaked her large nipples, "yours will be done soon as well"

"I don't want my nipples piercing mistress" I said

"What you want matters not to me, or Mistress Andrea, you will do as we say from now on and you will be our star attraction on the opening night at our club next week."

Andrea now completely removed the harness from my cock and balls and replaced it with a metal cage like contraption that fit around the base of my cock and encased it and my balls and fitted a small padlock.

Rosa said "Now that my sweet is a chastity device, it will allow you to pee but make sure you don't start to get an erection as it will be very painful"

They now swiftly released me from my restraints and told me to stand. "Now, on your knees and kiss my pussy and thank me for your evenings education" said Andrea brandishing her riding crop.

Not wanting to feel that again tonight I did as ordered. She immediately told me to do the same to "Mistress Rosa". Taking the hint I turned to my wife, kissed her pussy and said "Thank you for my education Mistress Rosa"

"Very good" said Andrea. "Now put on your robe and go home, make sure you get a good nights sleep, I want you back here in the morning 9:30 on the dot wearing nothing but your robe, ready to continue your training. Mistress Rosa will stay here tonight and you may well hear us pleasuring each other. I do hope that doesn't give you an erection as it would be very painful. One last thing" she said offering me a small blue diamond shaped tablet. "Make sure you take this pill just before you leave home in the morning, and I will know if you fail to take it so don't risk the consequences.

With that I put on my robe and Rosa led me to the door "see you in the morning slave" she said and shut the door behind me.

Forbidden Love (Rough Forbidden)

Feelings of love overcome guilt.

She knew it was wrong. It had been several weeks since she realized that she was having fantasies about a man who should have been entirely off-limits.....taboo. Josie was beside herself with what to do about her secret yearnings. The subject of her desire was her niece's live-in boyfriend, and herself being a married woman!

"My God," Josie thought, "Carol is like a daughter to me. I practically raised her. I'm like a second mom to her!"

Yet still, Josie could not quell the heat between her legs whenever she thought about the gorgeous hunk of male with whom her niece was in a relationship. Eric was his name.

"Eric," Josie sighed as she rubbed her overheated pussy lips through her tight-fitting jeans. Eric wasn't a big man height-wise, but more than made up for his lack of height by his good looks and a great-looking body. He had dark hair with piercing blue eyes, and always sported a great tan. He obviously took pride in his appearance, and of course, encouraged others around him to do so also. Eric worked out frequently and sported a killer set of pecs that just screamed Touch Me! Eric was also almost 20 years older than Carol, making him just 2 years younger than Josie herself.

He was friendly towards Josie in the beginning, not overly friendly, but not shy. He was the kind of guy who made sure everyone was comfortable and well taken care of as a guest in his home. Josie seemed to spark some little bit of chemistry within him too, she thought. Their eyes would seek out each other's out across a room, as if to confirm some deep secret . Eric was still attentive and outwardly devoted to Carol, but as time went on, passing comments with double-meanings would start to slip into their conversations. Everyone would always giggle, but when their eyes met, they could both tell maybe something else was there. Something perhaps real?

Gradually their friendship started growing. Josie began finding more reasons to call her niece or go over to their home. At first Josie felt maybe she was just imagining things, until Carol called her and started telling Josie the compliments that Eric was saying about her. It was at a mini family reunion when the first of such "compliments" came back to Josie, with Carol reporting that Eric said, "Man, your aunt sure looked HOT today!" Josie glowed inwardly at the comment. At another family gathering not too much later after that, he was also reported to have said that Josie looked gorgeous in her dress.

Josie inwardly smiled at the thought of his gaze being upon her...looking appreciatively at her voluptuous curves. Josie, while never being model-thin, had been through some rough times with depression and a difficult phase in her marriage in the last few years, and had put on quite a few extra pounds. She had felt in recent months a why-bother kind of attitude towards her weight, but upon learning his comments, Josie started to reassess her thinking. Maybe it was time to start her make-over and convert herself into the truly stunning creature she could be. Josie had always boasted a big bust throughout her puberty and adult life. Even as a teen, she had size 36C breasts, but as the years and gravity took over, she had reached a bra size of 40D. Her nipples almost always stood out, erect and proud, with big areolas surrounding them about the size of a half dollar. They were light pink/brown in color, and became even darker when she tanned on a regular basis. Standing at 5 feet 4 inches, frosted blonde hair, Josie felt, besides her blue eyes, her breasts were probably the best feature she had.

One afternoon Josie received a call from Eric, asking for her assistance. He needed to go out for an appointment, but Carol was not yet back and someone needed to be there to watch their child. Josie was the only person he could think of at the moment to call. She was delighted to be able to help out. When she reached their home, she noticed worry lines about Eric's eyes. Josie asked what was up, and he sighed and said, "I don't know. Carol's doing her own thing lately, and I have no idea what that is. I really can't say anything, because I don't know what's wrong."

Josie wanted to reach out to him, but refrained and instead said, "That doesn't sound good at all."

"I know," he answered. Then he shook his head and said, "But I don't want to bring someone else into our problems."

Their eyes locked for several moments. Josie could feel the tension and felt she should do something, but just then Eric shook his head and walked into the other room getting his car keys and giving instructions as to where everything was.

"I should only be gone maybe half hour to an hour. I can't thank you enough for helping out."

"My pleasure," Josie said. "It's the least I can do for all the things you've done for me in the last few months."

Eric gathered himself up and left for his appointment. This gave Josie time to think. She definitely knew there was something going on with her niece. She was up to something, and because of Carol's past history with men and promiscuity, Josie feared the worst. Eric was so loving and so good to her. We all felt Carol was finally getting her life together, found a good man, and now this. Josie was torn. On one hand, she wanted Carol and Eric to make it. They made a very handsome couple indeed, and she seemed to be settling down happily, especially since the birth of their child. On the other hand, if Carol and Eric split up, that might make it easier for her to explore her feelings for Eric. What to do....what to do.

A short while later, Eric returned. He looked a little bit better, having gotten a hair cut and some necessary errands out of the way. Josie greeted him with her best "neutral" smile. He sighed again and said, "Carol called me on my cell. She's pissed because I called you to come over."

Josie shook her head. She offered, "You know, if you want to talk, I've got great ears and broad shoulders."

Eric smiled sadly and said, "Thanks, but I really wouldn't know what to say at this point. How about a hug though?"

Josie stepped forward and embraced him fully, feeling her generous breasts crushed against his hard muscular chest. They held each other for several moments before he broke contact and cleared his throat. His eyes were not quite watery, but looked on the brink. Josie felt it was probably best if she left now before she made a move that might prove to be more than either of them could resist. Josie picked up her purse and keys, and told him, "If you ever need someone, I'll be here for you."

"I know. And thank you," answered Eric.

The next few weeks passed without any more tense moments or touching, just quite a few "oh by the way, I needed to call you because..." phone calls. Josie and Eric both made reasons to call each other for advice on this or that. Of course, their conversations always led to other subjects.

One evening Josie was talking with Carol and thought of a computer question. With Carol being completely ignorant of anything computer-related, she passed the phone over to Eric. Josie asked her question which was very easily answered by Eric, and as usual, their conversation went on to other things. Somehow Josie let it slip that she had started working out in the gym again. This seemed to please Eric very much. He said, "I'm so glad you're doing this Josie. It won't be anytime at all before you're the stunningly beautiful person I know you can be. You're so pretty now, I bet you're absolutely gorgeous when you're at your ideal weight."

Josie felt a warm flush to her cheeks listening to his words, and an even warmer feeling creeping along the insides of her thighs and higher. She answered, "Yes, I'm going to be that mean, lean, sex machine I once was!"

"OH MY GOD!" Josie thought. "I can't believe I just said that to him."

Eric just chuckled and said, "When you get to your goal, I'll tell you, Carol and your husband better watch out! Your husband teases you now about me being your boyfriend...I might not mind that at all!"

Josie looked at the phone, stunned! She answered, "You got that right, BoyFriend! I may be married, but I'm not dead!"

Eric chuckled and said, "I better stop talking. Something's 'stirring' around here and I might get myself in trouble," chuckling again.

They hung up the phone, Josie hugging herself and feeling on top of the world. Yes!!! Now she knew. Now he knew too! Her questions were finally answered. "Now what am I gonna do?" Josie asked herself.

Her next opportunity to see Eric came quite unexpectedly the next week. Josie's tanning facility was undergoing renovations and she had been having to use the store across town next to the gym where Eric worked out. She was just coming out from a tanning session when she spotted Eric on his way into the gym.

"Hey there handsome," she said. Eric stopped and turned her way. She was greeted with a broad smile that lit up his entire face.

"Hi sexy! Fancy meeting you here," Eric replied.

Josie told him about the remodeling going on and why she was on this side of town. Eric seemed lost in thought for a moment, then said, "Well, I was going to work out for a bit, but I did want to talk to you about something. Do you think we could go over to the bar/grill at the hotel across the street, and I can buy you lunch instead?"

"Sure that would be fantastic," Josie replied.

They jumped in their respective cars and drove across the avenue to the hotel restaurant. Josie and Eric walked up to the hostess and were seated within a few minutes at a very private booth towards the back of the restaurant. They placed orders for drinks and the waitress moved away to get them.

Eric suddenly turned to Josie and grasped her hands in his. He looked deep into her eyes and that was when she noticed a slight sheen of tears forming in his.

"Tell me Eric. What is it? What is wrong?" Josie asked.

"It's Carol," he choked out. "She's leaving me. I can't believe it, she's leaving me for a damned monkey ass!" he blurted out. His eyes threatened to overflow with his tears.

"Oh, no!" Josie cried. "I'm so sorry Eric. I had no idea your situation had deteriorated so far." Instinctively, she reached over and pulled him closer to her, into her arms. They hugged for a moment, then seemingly of their own volition, their bodies drifted closer and closer. Josie was murmuring soft reassurances into Eric's ear, and he was breathing deeply, trying to gain control of his emotions.

Josie was warring with her deeply felt feelings for him, and her family ties with Carol. On one hand, she had a gorgeous hunk of a man in her arms, holding her, needing her, but on the other hand, she was Carol's flesh and blood Aunt. Josie was so furious with Carol at this moment...furious with her for hurting this fine man, and furious for destroying yet again another relationship in a long list of failed relationships and destroyed lives that she had created in her short life. Josie decided to opt for the here and now. Eric needed her, and Lord knows, she needed him, desperately.

Not wanting to break contact with him, Josie started stroking Eric's neck and head, running her fingers through his hair, massaging his tense muscles. She felt him start to relax and loosen up under her ministrations. Feeling a little bolder, Josie nuzzled closer in his neck and gave him several little soft kisses behind his ear. She felt and heard Eric moan softly, and his hands and arms started to subtly change their motions. Instead of just clinging to Josie, Eric started to return her stroking and massaging. He lifted his head from her shoulder so he could look into her eyes. There, seated at the table, still embracing each other, their eyes met. An electric jolt went through both their bodies and they knew. There was a desire, a feeling so strong, that neither of them could deny it.

At that moment, the waitress returned with their drinks. Josie and Eric both decided to forego any meal, finished their drinks, and got up to pay the check. Instead of going to their cars, however, Eric took Josie by the hand, and guided her over to the registration desk in the adjoining hotel. With no words needing to be spoken, he paid for a room and they went up the elevator to their room.

Once inside their room, Eric and Josie ran into each other's arms and kissed, passionately, deeply, and with raw emotion. Their lips met and parted, with tongues dancing in each other's mouths. Josie had never felt such an intense feeling in all her life. She started to quickly remove her clothing, but Eric stopped her.

"No," he said. "I want to do it. I want to do it slowly and savor every moment, every inch of your luscious body. I've wanted to do this for a very long time, but I felt you were so off bounds because you're married and Carol's aunt."

"Hush," Josie replied. "None of that matters. I haven't been happy in my marriage in a long time, and Carol obviously doesn't care about you and your relationship since she is so willing to throw it away on this other jerk. I love you Eric. I've loved you for a very long time."

With that said, Eric smiled broadly probably for the first time in months. He reached over and softly cupped her face in his hands and lightly kissed her on the lips. His hands slowly slid down to her blouse and began to unbutton it. One by one the buttons came open, revealing her nude colored, lacy bra. It was sheer enough to where he could see her pert nipples through the material. He slipped the blouse off her shoulders and she allowed it to fall to the floor. Next, he undid the button and zipper on her pants, and slowly slid them down her smooth, tanned legs. When he got to her feet, she stepped out of them, and Eric tossed them to the side. Josie was now standing in only her lacy bra with matching thongs, having tossed off her sandals when her pants were removed. Eric stood back up, raking his fingers along her skin on the trip back up. Josie's skin felt like it was on fire where he touched her. He brought every nerve ending to life. His eyes feasted on her body for a long time before he moved again. He stepped closer to Josie, took her in his arms, and kissed her deeply and thoroughly. He wound his fingers in her hair, and pulled lightly, making Josie gasp a little and open her mouth. He took advantage and slid his hot tongue inside, probing the depths of her hot mouth, their passion mounting by the second.

He slid his hands downward and unhooked the bra from the back, and stepped back. Eric slid one strap from her shoulder, and then the other. Josie shrugged the rest of the bra off, and offered her ample sized 40D breasts to him. He leaned forward and slowly licked and sucked around her areolas, first one side and then over to the other side, until both nipples stood out proud and erect, glistening wet with his saliva. Josie had always had very sensitive breasts and nipples, and so she moaned and threw her head back, enjoying every last lick.

"Oh God, Eric," she sighed. "I never knew it could be this wonderful." She arched her back even more, aching for him to take her nipples back into his mouth, her need for him growing ravenous.

Eric proceeded to lick and suck some more, massaging both breasts, then nibbling lightly. He slowly licked his way around both breasts thoroughly and the proceeded to lick his way down her belly, to her belly button. There he paused again, licking in and around her navel, causing shivers of delight and anticipation in Josie. As his exploration of her body continued, Eric slowly sank to his knees, and proceeded to peel down her lacy thongs. As he did so, the strong scent of her arousal could be smelled, filling his senses, and driving him further in his need to have her. His tongue burned a path from her belly, down to her neat patch of hair just above her swollen pussy lips. Josie could hardly stand by this time, shaking in her desperate need for him to take her. Eric, sensing her impatience, decided to give her a little sample of what was in store for her. His tongue darted around her love bud, licking up and down her lips, diving once or twice into her hot, juicy pussy, but never directly hitting on her love button. Josie started to grab him by the hair and guide his mouth to her desired destination, but instead, Eric stood up and started to finger her pussy. She was so wet, his finger slid easily inside her. He plunged his finger in and out and in and out, making Josie practically hump his finger seeking relief. He then inserted a second, and then a third finger into her starving hole. This new invasion into her pussy sent Josie spiraling into her first orgasm. She grabbed a hold of Eric's shoulders, eyes rolled back into her head, and her whole body shuddered with ecstasy.

When Josie's breathing became more normalized, Eric held her, and kissed her deeply again. He took her by the hand and guided her over to the bed. There, he sat Josie on the edge of the bed, and stood between her open legs. He lowered himself down to his knees once more, and immediately dove into her hot, steaming pussy with his tongue. He was ravenously hungry...hungry for her taste. His tongue darted everywhere, lapping her exquisitely distended clit, licking her juices, and plunging his tongue into her hot, steamy pussy. He could not get enough of her taste. She had the most sexy aroma when she was aroused, and he wanted to drink every drop of her elixir. He continued licking, sucking, and teasing her clit, then inserting one or two fingers into her tight pussy and started to finger fuck her. When his finger was well lubricated, he removed it from her pussy and slid it down towards her ass. When he gently probed at her anus and found no resistance on her part, he inserted his fingertip. This, combined with his talented tongue on her clit, sent Josie over the edge once again, and she collapsed back on the bed in another mind-blowing orgasm. She spasmed and jumped all over, humping his tongue and fingers, grabbing his hair, and screaming out his name.

As Josie was peaking in this magnificent climax, Eric stood over her, and inserted his very hard, very excited 8 inch cock deep inside her quivering pussy. She was so wet he was met with no resistance, and was easily accepted all the way up until he met her cervix. Unknowingly, Eric had just performed the greatest turn-on he could ever have done for Josie. She loved having a hard cock slammed into her just as she was cumming hard, and she was loving every second of this. After a few minutes of hard and fast fucking, Eric slowed his pace, wanting to savor every moment, every feeling, every expression on Josie's beautiful face and body.

Eric was such a loving and patient lover she discovered. He had staying power well beyond any lover she had ever experienced, and seemed to know instinctively what she wanted, or needed, and anticipated her every desire. Josie went on to cum over and over again, under the expert loving and care of Eric. Eventually, Eric could contain himself no more, and once again increased his tempo, feeling his load building stronger behind every thrust. Josie could feel his balls tightening and his cock swelling and anticipated his ejaculation. When she felt him begin to release, she squeezed his cock with her tight pussy muscles, milking every drop from his rod, and loving the pulsations and feeling of fulfillment she was experiencing.

Eric collapsed on the bed beside her, his cock still inside her, as they both lay there, looking into each other's eyes. Josie smiled at Eric and he grinned back. They knew this was just the beginning of something very special.

Forbidden and Explicit Erotica for Adults

The craziest stories you've ever read. Orgy and couple swapping that you don't even know

This is a work of fiction. Names, character, places and incidents are either the product of the author's imagination or are used fictitiously, and any resemblance to actual persons, living or dead, business establishments, events or locales is entirely coincidental.

@ COPYRIGHT BY Jessica Dominate

All right reserved. No part of this book may be reproduced or used in any manner without written permission of the copyright owner except for the use of quotation in a book review.

Joy & Norm's Party (Gangbangs)

Joy & Norm have a party at their house.

Joy and I decided to have a party at our house one evening The night of the party, Joy was still getting ready when people started arriving and when she came out of the bedroom, even I had to whistle! Joy was dressed to kick ass. She was wearing an almost sheer, very low cut blouse, her tits were clearly visible and her nipples were very noticeable through the thin material and she was not wearing a bra. Barely covering her pussy and ass, she had on a short, I guess you could call it, mini skirt and no panty's!

I guess I should tell you a little about Joy. She is 51 years old, 5'3", 115#, hazel eyes, blond, only on the top though, as she keeps her pussy hair neatly trimmed, 36c-27-37. She likes her nipples licked on, sucked on and played with and they are the size of a dime when they are hard. Joy loves oral sex, both giving and receiving and she does swallow. Joy is into, incest, she fucks her oldest son, Jeff, eats her daughter, Dee's pussy, fucks her nephew Mark and her niece, Teri and eats her daughter-in-law, Maria's pussy, gangbangs, just about anything except S/M and pain and she is bi.

About 9 pm, I was getting a little tipsy already and I sat down on the couch next to Fred, a middle aged black guy. He was a little drunk by then also and we started casually talking, when Joy came up and ask me where another bottle of Canadian Club was, I told her and she winked and Fred and I, smiled and she left to get the bottle of booze. Fred couldn't help but stare at Joy's beautiful tits and after she left, he said that Joy was beautiful and had very nice tits and he would love to get her in bed and he thought she would be a very hot piece of ass and a great fuck.

Little did he know how right he was. We talked for a while longer before I got up to go get me another drink. Joy was outside on the deck talking with her daughter, Dee, her niece, Terry, her daughter-in-law Maria and a few others. I could see that she was having a pretty good time and she was a little drunk too. Joy had one hand on Maria's ass, rubbing Maria's ass cheeks and I knew that Joy was getting horny. I remembered what Fred had told me and got an idea.

I ask Joy to come here for a minute and when she did, I told her that some black guy had said she was beautiful, had great tits and that he would love to get her in bed because he thought she would be a great piece of ass and a great fuck. Joy smiled at me and ask if it were the black guy I was sitting with earlier and I told her that is was. Her eyes light up and she ask me if she should come on to him.

I told her that that was for her to decide and that it was fine with me if she did and if that was what she wanted. She smiled at me, gave my cock a little squeeze and told me to wish her luck. I looked at her and told her that she did not need any luck and that she would more than likely get lucky! Joy said something to the girls and went into the house. I went over to Maria and started talking to her and before long, she was rubbing my cock through my jeans. I whispered into ear if she would like to go into the bedroom, I sure would like a blowjob.

She smiled and gave my cock a big squeeze and I ask her if that was a yes. She smiled at me, gave my cock another squeeze and I reached up and took her tit in my hand, gave it a squeeze and told he to cum on. As we were going through the living room, Joy was setting next to Fred and she had her hand on his leg. I told Maria to hold on for just a minute, I wanted to see what Joy was going to do. She told me ok, so we stood next to Joy and Fred, listening to them talking.

Joy leaned over enough so that Fred could look down her blouse and see her tits. She smiled at him and ask him if he liked what he seen. Fred was having a hard time, Maria and I both could see a bulge in his pants, but answered Joy, that yes he did and they were lovely. Then Joy ask him if he would like to see all of them and Fred almost fell off the couch! Joy told Fred to watch her and in a minute or two to follow her into the bedroom.

The sweat broke out on Fred's forehead. As Joy got up and slowly walked to our bedroom, making sure that Fred was certain to see what room she went into. As soon as Joy got into the bedroom, she tore her cloths off and was standing there waiting for Fred, she reached over and turned the light off and was moving to get on the bed when Fred came in, he didn't notice yet that Joy was naked because his eyes were not yet accustomed to the darkness. Joy whispered to him to lock the door and moved nearer to him.

Fred turned and locked the door and when he turned around, Joy came up to him, wrapped her arms around his neck, pulled him to her and gave him a big, wet kiss. Fred nearly collapsed, but returned Joy's kiss. He still didn't realize that Joy was naked yet! Joy started unbuttoning his shirt as they continued kissing and when she had it unbuttoned, she pushed it off his arms and let it fall to the floor. She then pulled herself tight to Fred and it was then that Fred realized that Joy was topless and her beautiful tits were mashed to his chest!

Joy reached to Fred's pants and unbuckled than, reached for his zipper and unzipped his pants and pushed them off him and let them fall to the floor. Fred stepped out of them and was standing there in just his socks and underwear. Joy reached down and took his socks off and on her way back up, hooked her thumbs in Fred's underwear and began taking them off. Fred's cock got caught in the elastic band, so Joy had to pull his underwear out and down and when she did, out fell the biggest, blackest cock she had ever seen.

It had to have been at least 12 to 14 inch's long and thick! The thing was like a baseball bat. Joy just stared at Fred's cock! She couldn't believe the size of it. She took it in her hand and it didn't even come close to wrapping it around his cock. Joy knew right then that she had to have Fred's cock. She began stroking his cock, when Fred reached up and took Joy's tits in his hands and began squeezing and massaging them. Joy was already close to an orgasm and whispered in Fred's ear to get on the bed with her.

Joy led Fred by his cock to the bed and they laid down, Joy never letting go of Fred's cock. Joy kissed Fred again, still stroking his cock. She told Fred how bad she wanted his cock and could hardly wait to get it in her pussy and for him to fuck her. Fred began playing with Joy's tits again and took his other hand and moved it to Joy's pussy. Fred began massaging Joy's pussy and a low moan escaped from her. He slid one finger into Joy's wet pussy and began finger fucking her. Joy increased the speed of her strokes on Fred's cock.

Fred slid another finger into Joy's pussy and Joy had the first of her orgasms. Fred was close to cumming too and Joy, overcum with her own orgasm, didn't feel Fred's cock twitch and he shot a huge load of cum all over Joy and himself, gob after gob squirting from his cock. He couldn't believe the amount of cum he was spurting just from this sexy woman jacking him off! Joy, never let loose of his cock and her hand was covered with fresh, hot, creamy cum.

Joy ask Fred to fuck her now, but he had another idea. He told Joy that if she would suck his cock, then he would give her a fucking she would never forget! Joy wanted to suck his cock, but she wanted him to fuck her first, realizing that she would get that cock in her pussy sooner if she gave him a blow job, she began kissing his neck, slowly moving downward, stopping to lick and clean the cum from Fred's chest and belly.

Joy soon reached his hairline and the kinky, jet black hair was tickling her nose as she kissed lower and lower, finally reaching the base of Fred's cock. She began licking the long, hard, black shaft. When she licked down to the bottom of his cock, she started kissing and licking his balls.

Joy took one of Fred's nuts in her mouth and began sucking gently on it, before moving the other and doing the same with it, when she took Fred's cock in her hand and began stroking his cock again. She finally stopped licking and sucking his balls and began kissing and licking his cock up and down the shaft again. Fred took Joy's head in both hands, pulled it up over the head of his cock and pushed down. Joy's mouth reached the head of his cock and she opened her mouth as wide as she could and slid her mouth over the head of Fred's cock. Fuck, it was so big, she didn't think she could get anymore into her mouth, but Fred was still pushing and Joy was surprised she was getting so much of it in her mouth.

His cock finally hit the back of Joy's mouth and she began gagging a little. Fred let go of Joy's head and she began slowly bobbing her head up and down on as much of his cock as she could get in her mouth. Joy loved the warm, hard, black cock in her mouth. It was so hot and hard and big.

Joy took Fred's cock out of her mouth long enough to tell him how delicious it was and she was going to enjoy giving him a blow job and lowered her mouth back onto Fred's cock again and began sucking him off again. Joy knew that she had a mouthful of cock! Fred's cock felt so good as Joy's mouth slid up and down it, her lips wrapped tightly around Fred's cock!

Joy took Fred's balls in her hand and began squeezing and massaging them as she gently sucked on his cock, that huge hunk of meat lodged in her mouth, her head bobbing up and down, her tits swaying, jiggling and bobbing to the motions of her mouth on Fred's monster cock. Joy would stop every so often to lick the drops of precum that formed at the tip of Fred's cock and loved the taste of it, knowing that before long she was going to taste gobs and gobs of it, hopefully filling her belly with warm, gooey, creamy, delicious, sperm from this black man and his cock. When Fred started moaning, it was like music to Joy's ears.

She knew that Fred was close to blowing his load into her mouth and she was ready for it. Joy increased the speed of her head bobbing on Fred's cock, waiting for that delicious cum to start squirting into her mouth. She didn't have to wait long, with a grunt, Fred grabbed Joy's head and held it on his cock, Joy felt Fred's cock jerk and twitch and she knew that he was going to cum any second.

Fred suddenly yelled, "fuck Joy, here I cum, her I cum, owww, here I cum" and with one big twitch, the sperm came blasting out of Fred's cock into Joy's mouth. Joy was not nearly ready for the amount of cum that came shooting from Fred's cock! His load was tremendous. His first squirt was more than most men cum altogether! Joy had all could do just to swallow that first stream of sperm that came shooting out of his cock, stream after stream pouring from Fred's cock.

Swallowing as hard and as much as she could, Joy could not swallow it all. Cum started leaking out of the corners of her mouth, dripping off her chin, down onto her tits! With one final shot, a huge stream of sperm came blasting into Joy's mouth! With Fred's jerking and bucking from his cumming, Joy never took her mouth off his cock and as he lowered his hips back onto the bed, Joy kept his softening cock locked into her mouth.

She was not going to miss one drop of sperm from that beautiful cock. Joy had her mouth still on Fred's cock before she realized that it was not going to get completely soft and she was positive that she had milked every drop of sperm from Fred's cock, she let it slip from her mouth and she began licking what cum had gathered on Fred's cock and balls. When Joy was sure that she had cleaned his cock and balls off, she moved back up next to Fred and began scooping the sperm from her chin and tits, sticking her fingers into her mouth and cleaning the cum from them.

Once she had cleaned up every drop of sperm, she licked her lips, looked at Fred and ask him if that would do and how did he like it. Fred just looked at Joy and told her that he had never had his cock sucked that good and that she was the best cocksucker he had ever met and that the brothers would love to get her in a gangbang. Joy told Fred that she would love for him to arrange a gangbang with all his friends for her, but for now she wanted to fuck and they could talk about and make the arrangements later! Joy took his cock in her hand and started stroking it again and it wasn't very many strokes before she felt Fred's cock getting hard again.

She moved onto her back and told Fred to get on and bury that cock in her. Fred started to roll over and get on top of Joy, so she spread her legs as wide as she could while Fred got on her and she put Fred's cock up to her pussy and told him to fill her pussy with cock. There was a little resistance from the size of Fred's cock, but as wet as Joy's pussy was, it didn't take a lot before the head of Fred's cock slid into Joy's pussy. Fred stopped to allow Joy's pussy to get used to the size of his cock.

Within seconds, Joy told his to "cum on baby, give mama that cock, fill my pussy, ram it home baby and fill my pussy with black cock, don't wait baby, let me have it all now" and Joy lunged upwards until Fred's cock was buried deep in her pussy, his balls resting against her ass. She had taken every inch of his cock! They settled back down on the bed and Joy ask Fred to just lay still for a moment or two and let her feel his cock filling and stretching her pussy, to feel it's hardness, it's heat, it' size in her. Joy's pussy was filled with more cock than ever before and she knew that this was going to be a fantastic fuck.

Joy looked into Fred's eyes and told him "to fuck her right now" and he slowly started thrusting his cock in and out of her pussy. On the 4th stroke, Joy had another orgasm and started meeting each thrust with one of her own. She was in another world. He pussy filled with the biggest, blackest cock she had ever known of, stretching her cunt to limits she could not believe and she was loving it. Nothing else mattered to her except the cock that was pounding her pussy at that moment. Fred increased the speed of his thrusts, his balls slapping Joy's ass every time his cock buried itself in her pussy.

All Joy could do was moan, "oh fuck me, your cock is so wonderful, I'll never let you go, fuck me, fuck me, your cock feels so good filling my pussy, I'm so glad that you came to the party, fuck me Fred, fuck me, do you like fucking this old white woman?, I am your white whore weather you like it or not, I need your big, black cock, please don't ever stop fucking me, I love you and your cock, fuck me, please fuck me, harder, slam your cock in my pussy, use me as the slut I am now baby, fuck me, fuck me", Fred suddenly pulled his cock out and Joy screamed, "no, no, please put it back in" Fred told her to roll over and get on her hands and knees and Joy quickly did and as soon as she was in position, Fred moved in behind he and shoved his cock right back into Joy's pussy and began fucking her doggie style.

Joy taking every thrust, her tits bobbing and flopping wildly with each of Fred's thrusts, she reached her hand behind her and took Fred's ball's in them and began squeezing and massaging them. Freed could feel another load of sperm building in his balls and knew he was going to blast it into Joy's pussy soon, but kept pounding away at Joy's Pussy. Joy felt Fred's balls tighten up and gave then one big squeeze and the sperm litterly shot from Fred's cock, overfilling Joy's pussy. Fred gave one big lunge and drove every bit of his cock into Joy's pussy and Joy screamed as she felt it splashing against the walls of her pussy. Fred's cum and Joy's pussy juices were dripping out of her pussy and pooling on the bed.

They stayed like that for a few more minutes, letting the rush calm down before either moved, then they both collapsed onto the bed, Joy's pussy and legs, Fred's cock, balls and legs soaked with both their juices, sweat glistening from both their body's. They were both drenched. It was almost a full 5 minutes before either moved a muscle. Fred told Joy how great a fuck the she was and said it was too bad that they had not meet years ago and Joy told him how fantastic a fuck he was and her pussy had never had so much or as big a cock as his and how much she loved it and hoped that he was serious about getting his friends together with her for a gangbang. He told her that he was very serious and that he would start on it the first thing in the morning and he would call her when he had it all set up.

He ask her if she had anyplace in mind and Joy ask him if her house would be ok. Fred ask he why her house and Joy told him that that way, all the guys there would know where she lived in case they ever wanted to cum over and fuck her again. Fred agreed that it was a good idea and ask her how soon she would be able to have them cum over. Joy ask him how soon he could get them together and bring them over and ask him if the next night would be ok. Fred told her that he would get as many of his friends together and he would bring them over tomorrow night.

That got Joy horny again. She took Fred's semi hard cock in her hand and began stroking it and after a dozen or so strokes, she felt Fred's cock rising again. Joy kept her hand on his cock, rose up and squatted over Fred's cock, lowered her pussy to the head of his cock and plunged all the way down onto it and screamed as it hit bottom. Fuck, it felt like it was jammed clear up to her throat, from the inside! What a cock that man had and he was letting Joy have her way with it.

Up and down Joy rode his monster cock! Her tits were flopping wildly and Fred just stared at them, only taking his eyes off them long enough to see his cock disappearing into Joy's cunt every time she slammed down onto him. He could not get over this white woman riding his cock. Fuck she was good and he was amazed how easily she took every inch of his cock. Joy was the first white woman that had ever taken it all. They had been fucking for over three hours and Joy wanted more! He was very glad that he had come to the party now as he lay there, letting Joy fuck him.

He could not get over how good pussy she was. Fred had fucked other white women before, but none could come close to the one fucking him now and none had ever sucked his cock before, let alone swallow his cum. And the same was true for Joy. She had fucked other black men, but none could come close to the size or stamina of the cock she was riding and had filling her pussy! Fred began to feel that familiar tingling in his balls that he knew Joy was leading to him blasting another load of cum in Joy's pussy and he told Joy that he was going to pop a nut again soon. Joy could feel another orgasm building in her and she began riding Fred faster and harder. Fred reached up and took Joy's flopping tits in his hands and that did it for Joy!

The orgasm hit her hard and she sank all the way down on Fred's cock and couldn't move, it was as if she was impaled on Fred's cock, shuddering as the orgasm overtook her while Fred let loose with huge shots of sperm. Joy could feel her pussy getting filled with shot after shot of Fred's warm sperm and that only added to her throngs of passion. The orgasm lasted for a full two or three minutes and when it subsided, Joy collapsed onto Fred and just lay on top of him.

Suddenly and for some reason, it struck Joy that there were hardly any sound, except for the music, coming from outside the bedroom and she became very curious as to why. Fred was laying there with his eyes shut, when Joy mentioned that to him. She told him that maybe they should take a short break and rejoin the party and if he wanted, they could come back into the bedroom in a short while. Joy rolled off of Fred and gave a big sigh when his cock slipped out of her pussy, but if she had her way, it would not be long before it was filling her mouth and pussy again and she told Fred just that and he looked into her eyes and told he that he sure hoped that would be the case.

They got off the bed and got dressed and started to leave the bedroom. The sight that met them was amazing and they had to step back for a moment. There were people all over the house having sex. It was a full blown orgy! Joy looked around for Norm and finally found him on the floor in the living room. Maria was sucking his cock and he was eating some big titted brunette's hairy pussy. The sight was awesome. Dee was getting fucked by two guys and jacking off another. Teri was eating some woman's pussy while some guy was popping the cock to her. The rest of the people were in various stages of fucking and or sucking cock or eating pussy.

No one noticed them come out of the bedroom and Joy told Fred to go back into the bedroom, they would get undressed and come back out and join in and they would fuck and suck among the others. They went back into the bedroom and then Joy got an idea. Why didn't Fred call some of his friends from there and see how many he could line up for the gangbang. Fred agreed and started calling them. As soon as he started calling, Joy reached and grabbed his cock and began stroking it.

As soon as she felt it getting hard, she knelt down in front of Fred and began sucking his cock. She took her mouth off his cock and ask him if he would tell them that the woman for the gangbang was sucking his cock right at this moment and Fred did just that. It was exciting for Joy, her lover asking his friends if they wanted to come to a gangbang with a white woman while she was sucking his cock.

Every one of Fred's friends agreed and he would bring them to Joy's that evening and Fred had only called eight of them. Fred finally hung the phone up and looked down at Joy's head bobbing on his cock, closing his eyes and savoring the pleasure Joy was administrating ton his cock and he knew that before long, he would fill her mouth and belly with another load of sperm. Joy had her hand on Fred's cock, stroking it as her head was bobbing on his monster cock and she grabbed his balls with her other hand and began rubbing and massaging them, hoping to get Fred to blow another load of sperm into her mouth.

Joy stopped sucking Fred's cock, looked up at him and told him that she wanted to go into the other room with him and let everyone watch her suck his cock and swallow his sperm when he squirted it into her mouth. Joy led Fred by his cock into the center of the living room, had him lay down on the floor and she get down between his legs, dropped her mouth onto his cock and started giving him another blow job. It wasn't long before Joy heard someone say, "fuck me, look at the size of the cock Joy is sucking, that thing is a monster"

Soon, everyone was watching Joy sucking Fred's monster cock and some started clapping and egging Joy on. Others were taking bets if she would swallow his cum or not. Maria in the meantime had stepped up to Fred and put her tit up to his mouth and he began sucking and nibbling on her nipples, first one then the other. Maria told everyone that when Joy was done sucking that cock, that it was hers next! Maria felt a hand on her pussy and when she looked to see whose it was, Joy already had two fingers in Maria's pussy and was finger fucking her frantically.

Joy took Fred's cock out of her mouth and told Dee to come and play with his balls while she was sucking his cock and that would make him cum that much sooner. Dee came over and took Fred's balls in her hand as Joy went back to sucking Fred's magnificent cock, It wasn't long before Dee began kissing and licking Fred's cock herself. That was too much for Fred to handle and without warning, he exploded into Joy's mouth. Joy, caught unexpectedly, started gagging, but never took Fred's cock from her mouth and began swallowing the sperm that was gushing into her mouth.

When Joy was sure that she had drained every drop of sperm from Fred's cock, she let it fall from her mouth and got up. A she did, Maria was kneeling in front of Fred and she was stroking his cock. Two guys grabbed Joy and led her to the couch and began mauling her. Their hands were all over her tits and pussy and she was getting turned on again! She knew that these guys would never come close to fucking her as good as Fred had, but the thought of someone fucking her and her sucking someone's cock at the same time was what got her horny again.

Fucking, sucking cock and eating pussy went on the rest of the night. As Joy and I were getting in bed, I started thinking of her sloppy, wet, well eaten, well fucked, sperm filled pussy. I had never eaten Joy's pussy after she had fucked anyone and her pussy was full of cum, but for some reason, eating her pussy right then excited me.

Joy laid down on the bed and I get between her legs and her eyes got big and she ask me what I was doing, but I never answered her and began licking and eating her pussy! The thought of me eating her cum filled pussy turned her on and her hips were rushing up to mash her pussy against my mouth as Joy had another orgasm. I crawled up next to Joy and we fell asleep in each other's arms.

Enjoying Threesomes (Threesome)

All combinations of 3 way sex - MMF, FFM MFstrapon.

*****

I hadn't been fucked, yet, but I had cum twice. Once when my husband Gordon finger fucked me as his friend Don kissed me and caressed my tits and secondly when Don nestled his deliciously thick and wonderfully hard cock in the cleft of my bum as he rubbed my clit and Gordon sucked my tits.

Gordon and I have been married for just three years; we have no children largely by choice, but also by age, he is fifty eight and I am forty nine. It is not a typical marriage, but then it is not an open one; perhaps slightly ajar might be the most apt description. Both of us occasionally slip through the open door to play away from home, but we never discuss what happens the other side of the door or ask questions. We both know that the other knows, but we never mention anything.

Like many men Gordon has a big thing for seeing two women together. Also he has big things for seeing me with another man and me seeing him with another guy or woman. Gordon is just about as bi as I am, see what I mean about it not being a typical marriage?

Gordon has a fine body. He's quite good looking, just over six feet and weighs around two hundred pounds. Although he works out regularly and plays tennis a couple of times a week his physique is showing the signs of age, but I do not mind that and in any case so is mine. I'm five six with long, black hair that would be flecked with streaks of grey if I did not attend to them. Generally I wear my hair down and probably a little too long for a woman of my age for it tumbles down over my shoulders and onto my back and chest. My body is ok, but there's a little extra padding round the hips and bum and my thighs could be slightly less chunky. Most people, particularly men, however, pay little attention to that for their gaze tends to be focused on my breasts. They are big. In UK measurements they are double D plus, in US sizes, fuck knows. So that's me. Oh yes I am as blind as a bat and do not get on well with contacts so I wear glasses, usually horn rimmed.

We were both aware of the other's 'biness' before we became partners and subsequently married. In fact when I met Gordon through work I was leading a fairly full on lesbian life style. At the time I was living in New York working for a global ad agency. He was a consultant advising us on what persuades people to buy products and knew the woman I was living with. He had known her for some time and one night the three of us ended up in bed. I was pleased to find that I had not become a hard core les as I enjoyed Gordon as much as I did Hayley. He was my first man for five years!

When I moved back to London we slowly got together and became a number. I am not sure whether it was an aid or a detriment to our relationship, but Gordon lived in Oxford where he lectured in applied psychology at the university and I moved into my parent's house in Barnsbury, north London. They had died a few years previously and it had been rented out whilst I was in the US. I had left the agency and was working freelance so that provided an ideal living and working space for me.

As we went through our 'courtship' we made 'confessions' to each other, but I never quite owned up to having lived the life of a lesbian for five years, although of course Hayley may have told him. Equally Gordon did not tell me about the numbers of men he had been with and just how deep into the Oxford gay and bisexual scene he was.

Nevertheless After a year or so we got married.

****

It was in one of those 'mellow moments' when we'd had terrific sex and were lying in each other's arms sharing a spliff and talking that he said.

"Well how about with another man?"

That excited me. The idea of making love to another guy as my husband watched was a surprisingly strong turn on.

"Would you join in or just watch?" I had asked taking a deep drag on the joint.

"Both, see how it goes" he replied.

However, nothing happened on that front for a few months.

Gordon was on business lecturing at MIT and we were in Boston staying in the Copley Marriott. I love New England generally and Boston in particular and I was tagging along for the ride and the great seafood. It was around nine in the evening when we were drinking in the bar. Gordon had to go to our room to send a contract from his laptop and I got chatting to a guy who had been sitting at the bar. Gordon joined us half an hour or so later.

We arranged to have dinner the next night and one thing led to another and we were in our suite having another drink before going into the bedroom and undressing. In the end they both fucked me and later I got them to wank each other. They came on my tits.

I got so turned on both by having sex with another guy in front of Gordon, but more so probably by seeing them masturbate each other. For some time after that my mind would wander back to seeing them holding each other's cocks, to looking at the expressions on their faces as they rubbed each other and as they made each other cum. I acknowledged to myself that I wanted more.

And I got it.

The second time we did it a few months later it was less spontaneous. Gordon could not think of a friend who we could involve; hardly surprising really when we had both agreed that the boys should play with each other as well as look after me. I was becoming more and more convinced lately that Gordon enjoyed the attentions of another guy in Oxford rather more than he let on to me and hence, I was not surprised when quickly after we had discussed using an 'escort' that he had lined it all up.

Again they both fucked me. At one time we tried doing it with Gordon from the back and Peter from the front both up my pussy, but it didn't work. In the end Gordon took my bum, which he'd had numerous times before and Peter had the front entrance.

Later I revelled in helping them suck each other, but neither came in the other's mouth; they reserved that for my tits and tummy.

And now we were doing it again. Don was divorced. We only knew him from the local pub that Gordon and I visited sometimes together and sometimes alone on a Friday evening. He and I got on well and if it hadn't been so quite close to home and he wasn't a mate of Gordon then he and I could well have gone further! It was rumoured that his wife had left him because she found him with another guy although that was not substantiated. Gordon managed to do that one evening, although he never fully explained how. He didn't also fully explain how he had broached the topic, but informed me that Don would like to join us. That excited me for I did fancy him and the idea of him and Gordon together was a massive turn on.

The three of us went to lunch at a local Italian one Sunday, drank just a little too much Frascati staggered back to our house and simply went to bed. I had been worrying as to how we would actually get it on when Don came round so Gordon orchestrating it with the boozy lunch first worked great. He took over when we got back to the house for no sooner were in it than he said.

"I have to make a few calls so why don't you two get to know each other better?"

"How do you mean?" Don asked.

Gordon smiled. "Well you are two consenting adults aren't you?"

The look on his face when he returned to the living room twenty or so minutes later to find us in each other's arms on a sofa kissing was a sight to behold and that made me love him even more, in my way. At first we stopped but Gordon said.

"Don't let me stop you."

"Are you sure?" Don asked.

"You bet your fucking life I am. You just carry on and let me watch."

Don and I got back to it and gradually we got bolder. We sank back on the sofa so he was half lying on me. The kisses became deeper with open mouths, sucking lips and plunging tongues. I was ruffling his long, greying hair and slipping my fingers inside his dark blue with yellow stripes shirt causing the buttons to pop open. He tentatively at first, but then more confidently as he found no resistance from me or Gordon cupped, squeezed and stroked my breasts and pinched my nipples. He slid his hand inside my scoop fronted top and rubbed my breast through the thin bra sending shivers of pleasure and desire through me. I reached out for the interestingly large and thrillingly hard lump that had been pressing into my leg for the last few moments. It felt good.

Glancing over Don's shoulder my eye caught Gordon's gaze. He smiled and nodded encouragingly looking down at where my hand was now rubbing Don's cock through his dark blue linen trousers.

Don scooped one of my boobs from the protection of the bra cup and mad the usual appreciative noises that I was no so used to hearing. He squeezed it nicely and pinched and pulled my nipple as he thrust his hard on more firmly against my hand. I took that as an invitation or a request and I slid his zip down. Surprisingly easily I got my hand inside his thin trousers and boxers and gripped the bare flesh of his dick.

"Oh yes Tina" he groaned into my ear as he eased my other boob out of my bra, rolling that and my top down so that both of my tits were bare.

It was getting pretty steamy when Gordon chimed in.

"Why don't we get a little more comfortable and use the bed?"

"Sounds good to me," Don replied sitting up.

"Tina why don't you go up and get ready for us?" Gordon suggested.

I left the two of them and went upstairs. Taking my bra and top off I fluffed up my black hair and checked myself in the mirror. Pleased with what I saw for my boobs, given their size do not sag that much and my tummy is childless flat. I slipped my skirt off and contemplated whether to keep my panties on or not; I had already decided to keep the lacy topped holdups on so I took the black thong off. After all it was an Agent Provocateur special and had cost a ridiculous amount considering how little there was of it; I didn't worry about the holdups getting damaged for they were just straightforward Wolfords at a tenner a pair.

Getting into the bed just under the sheet I waited for my lovers thinking. 'Where the bloody hell are they?'

They weren't much longer and they came in bearing wine and glasses, ashtrays and cigarettes and Gordon's tin containing the spliffs.

Standing at the foot of the bed where I could look at both of them they undressed. They both had good bodies with Gordon looking the fitter and leaner and Don having the bigger dick. Both were nicely hairy.

They lay either side of me and I kissed them both.

"Welcome," I smiled. "I thought you had changed your minds."

It was only a short time later that as I was kissing Don and he was rubbing my tits that Gordon caressed my pussy lips as a prelude to shoving his fingers up me and finger fucking me to that first, ice-breaking climax. That was quickly followed by Don making me cum from rubbing my clit as he nestled his cock between my bum cheeks making me wonder whether that was going to be used this evening?

We all messed around on the bed for some time. Rolling around with both of them kissing and caressing me it was a pretty much straightforward threesome I guess with me excitingly the centre of attention; for a while that was perfect. It was not long, though, before Gordon said.

"Go on Don fuck her, she's ready I can tell. Right Tina?"

"Mmmmmmm how did you guess?" I smiled back looking at Don and saying. "How do you want me Don?"

He fucked me from behind with me lying on my side kissing and being caressed by my husband. Don didn't take that long before cumming. As he pulled out, Gordon immediately shoved his cock in and fucked me hard and quick. It was quite some feeling to have an orgasm by one man that was transferred to another, especially as the second one was my husband!

We rested for a while. I could have gone on of course, but then women can can't we? But men? Especially early middle-aged men, they have to take time to recover.

We shared a joint, had a cup of tea, wandered naked around the house, had some cheese and biscuits and then started kissing and caressing again. They both quickly showed signs of recovering particularly when I placed their hands on the other's dick. I watched Gordon carefully and, as I suspected, directly Don started stroking his cock Gordon' reacted very quickly.

"That nice?" Don grunted.

"Mmm, smashing," Gordon sighed clearly pushing himself against Don's hand.

They were kneeling either side of me so I was able to join in. I stroked my way up their thighs and cradled a pair of balls in each hand.

I saw them looking intently at each other as both of them reached out with the hand that wasn't holding the other's cock. Don put his hand on Gordon' shoulder. Gordon seemed to welcome it and leaned forward as he slid his arm round Don's waist. I found it so exciting as I thought 'are they going to kiss?' And they were. It was incredible to see their bodies close the gap between them, their chests press together, their hands pump the other's cock and their mouths meet. My husband is kissing another man went through my mind as I squeezed both pairs of balls. Momentarily I felt a surge of jealousy for he seemed to be enjoying it a little too much in my opinion, but that passed as I got more into what they were doing. The jealousy vanished and was replaced by excitement.

I watched their mouths grinding and their lips squirming as undoubtedly their tongues plundered inside the other's mouth. Their hands started to roam over the other's body and although they couldn't get to their cocks, for I was holding them they went up and down their backs and onto their bums.

I was realising that I was becoming rather redundant, but so excited was I becoming at seeing Gordon and Don getting it on that I didn't mind.

"You ok with this?" Gordon asked me.

"Yes," I whispered alternating my hands between stroking their cocks and balls and rubbing my tits and pussy lips.

"And are you Gordon?" Don asked as they broke their kiss.

"Yes. Yes I am Don, are you?"

Don beamed a broad smile. "Oh yes Gordon, very, very much so."

"Good," my husband replied in a taught sounding voice.

Don backed away coming nearer to me. I took that to mean he was offering me his cock so I leaned forward, pulled it towards me and kissed it. He was now fully hard so I took him into my mouth.

"Mmmmm lovely Tina that's great, but what about Gordon?"

I slipped the dick out of my mouth and looking at Gordon first then at Don I croaked. "Well why don't you look after him Don, I'm sure Gordon will be ok, won't you darling.

He nodded. Don leaned forward and taking Gordon' cock in his hand he licked his length before doing to my husband exactly what I was doing to him, sucking his cock in long, greedy gulps. I had of course seen Gordon being sucked before, but that didn't detract from the excitement and pleasure I gained this time. With my mouth full of Don and one hand cradling his balls I reached out with the other and after stroking Gordon' balls I held his cock as Don licked and sucked it. This freed up Don's hands and they almost immediately found my tits that I gratefully pushed towards them. He pinched my nipples wonderfully. We kept on like that for a while until Gordon wanted his turn so we switched round and I sucked him as he sucked Don. I was holding Don's prick so they both had free hands and I revelled in having four hands groping and caressing me.

For some reason we suddenly stopped. I don't know why? I was sitting up between them where they were kneeling looking at each other.

"Well Gordon?"

I could see the apprehension in Gordon' eyes as he pondered on what Don meant, just as I was.

"Sorry," Gordon muttered.

"I meant what now Gordon?"

"What do you mean?" Gordon stammered.

"I would have thought that was simple, what do you want now?"

"Oh dear" Gordon smiled looking from Don to me and back again.

"What?"

"I don't know."

"How do you mean? You don't know what I mean or what you want?"

"Both I guess."

"I see" Don said looking at me. "And what about you Tina?"

I truly didn't know what he meant when he addressed me, although I suspect Gordon knew perfectly well that Don was asking him whether he wanted to fuck or be fucked. My heart was pounding at the thought.

"What about me Don?" I asked stroking his nicely rounded bum.

"What would you like is to do now."

"You and Gordon?"

"Yes."

Looking at my husband I said in a croaking voice. "Whatever you both want to do."

Smiling at me, Don looked at Gordon and said quietly.

"Back in your court then Gordon."

"Yes I see, but I really don't know. What would you like to do."

"The truth?" Don asked again looking at me as if for confirmation. I nodded and smiled encouragingly.

"Of course."

Don moved closer to Gordon, ran the back of his fingernails across his chest, let his hand wander downwards onto his cock, stroked that and then looking right into my husband's eyes said quietly.

"I would like to fuck you Gordon."

His words exploded into my mind. They were as exciting and erotic as I had ever heard. I gasped. Gordon looked at me and I nodded.

"Well Tina?" He asked. "Ok?"

"Yes darling" I breathed.

"Yes Don please fuck me" Gordon replied.

"Got some lube Tina?"

"KY ok?" I replied leaning over and opening my little toy drawer that contains a couple of vibrators, the little metal balls, condoms, almond and baby oils and the jelly; an advantage of not having children I smiled.

"That'll be fine."

I handed it to him.

"Why not lay on your front Gordon and get ready for me" Don said.

I sat beside Gordon' head as Don took the KY jelly and smeared it over Gordon' bum making him jump and sigh. He took a condom from the door. "Ok Tina?"

"Yes of course," I replied watching him slide it onto his cock.

"Ok darling?" I asked Gordon stroking his hair and feeling such powerful love for him. I couldn't understand how I could feel that when he was about to be fucked by another man, but I did.

Don got behind Gordon and taking hold of him by each hip he whispered.

"Kneel up for me a little Gordon, it'll be easier like that."

Gordon raised his bum, but kept his knees and head on the bed. I wanted to part of this. I wiggled closer and lifted his head and rested it in my lap. His arms went round me and pulled my tummy tighter to his face, he kissed it.

"Ready Gordon?" Don asked positioning himself between my husband's slightly parted legs. He was holding his condom covered cock about horizontal to the bed. It was nearly touching Gordon bum.

"Yes Don" Gordon said as I felt his grip tighten on the flesh on my hips just above my buttocks.

It really was an incredible sight to watch Don move the tip of his cock inside the crease of Gordon' bum, presumably right on his anus. I saw him push his hips a little and grip Gordon' hip tighter with his spare hand.

"Ok?" He asked.

Gordon grunted what sounded like a yes before gasping and saying sharply. "Oh fuck" as his fingernails dug into me. I stroked his face and whispered. "I love you Gordon."

"Ok Gordon" Don said rubbing his back. "

I didn't see Don move for a moment or two and then I saw him edge his hips forward a little. Gordon again gasped and cried out. We both reassured him. Don slowly edged himself further into Gordon until I could see he was in as far as he could go.

Gordon didn't react any more, but simply lay against me very tense as I held him. I could remember that feeling very well from when I first had full anal sex. Although we had never discussed, it the concern that Gordon displayed at being fucked suggested to me that he was probably a top and was used to fucking, but not being fucked.

"OK Gordon?" Don asked leaning forward and running his fingers through Gordon's hair.

"Yes."

"It's getting easier?"

"Yes it is."

"Want more?"

"Yes Don."

"What do you want now Gordon?"

"More."

"My cock is up you as far as I can get it Gordon."

"Good."

"So what do you want me to do now that I have got my cock as far up your arse as I can get it?"

I waited on my husband's answer enjoying the dirty talk that is often a feature of our lovemaking.

"Fuck me," Gordon whispered.

"Louder," Don ordered quite firmly slapping the bum in which his cock was buried.

"Fuck me Don, I want you to fuck me."

And that is precisely what Don did to my husband as I lay with them while Gordon grunted, groaned and moaned until Don made him cum all over my legs.

***

Things were much more out in the open after that episode. Gordon told me that he was mainly a top and that prior to that Sunday with Don he had only been fucked once before.

Our marriage settled into a pattern. We lived apart and got together every two to three weeks usually with Gordon visiting me, but occasionally with me going to Oxford. There was little opportunity for us to indulge ourselves with other women or men, but we had a great two day long session with Hayley when she came and stayed with me and we met with Don again where this time they both fucked me. Although Gordon said that he preferred being a top he had enjoyed being topped by Don so he let him do that again, but also I had the thrill of watching my husband fuck another man.

It was Gordon's birthday. He was coming to stay and we were going to a show in the West End, then dinner at Joe Allens before back to Barnsbury undoubtedly for a big night of sex. I had prepared for helping celebrate his birthday in my bed. When we got back to the house we had a drink and I suggested that he go upstairs and get in bed and told him I would be join him shortly.

I let him get up there and in the bathroom until I heard the shower running before creeping upstairs and into one of the spare bedrooms. I undressed and got ready.

"Mmmm you look lovely," Gordon said as he looked me up and down in my long, black silk and lace peignoir.

He was naked laying on the bed with the duvet pushed back.

"Thanks baby," I cooed walking over to the bed.

"Apart from looking fucking sexy, why have you got that on?" He asked sitting up.

I put one knee on the bed and fumbled with the tie at the waist of the robe. I undid it watching carefully the direction Gordon's gaze. It was focused fully on my body. Slowly without moving my gaze from him for one second I pulled the robe open.

"For this reason darling," I whispered sliding my hand down. "To cover this until I was ready," I went on stroking the thin, black plastic strapon. "Will you be my bottom Gordon.

House Call (BDSM)

She hires male prostitute for BDSM.

I arrive wheeling a metal case. I placed it on the table and opened it up. Inside were all manner of tools for the BDSM enthusiast.

Blindfolds, whips, chains and handcuffs. A collar and ball gag for the more noisy women, enough for some interesting fun. Also were a rope, a spreader bar, and all the apparatus for a BDSM sling included. She was decidedly brave to take all this on, on her first encounter but I supposed jumping into the deep end certainly had its advantages.

"I'll go and get changed in my bedroom, while you set up here." She said to me. She headed off to her bedroom and I began to set up. Her lounge was large and spacious. There were wrought iron bars on the windows. She also had a stripper pole, which came in handy later that day.

I attached the handcuffs to the bars. I then constructed the sling. Then I placed all the other apparatus on the table. The whips, collars, additional handcuffs, ball gag, the spreader bar, blindfold and containers of wax with a lighter next to it.

I limbered up and prepared for the festivities. I put on a large coat with a hood, leather gloves on my hands, military boots on my feet, metal cock ring and prepared for the fun to come. I knocked on her bedroom door "Come in" she said. I stepped inside.

She was standing there in four-inch black leather stiletto heels a shiny leather corset that stopped before her luscious 34C breasts and before her luscious beautifully shaved cunt. She was wearing arms length black leather gloves.

"Are you ready to begin madam?" I said rather formally.

"But of course" she cordially replied.

There was a distinctive deep clack of her heels as she moved across the wooden floor. It was silenced when she stepped onto the carpet. She looked around at the various BDSM devices I had set up.

Her heart sped up a few beats and her breathing became more audible. She was excited and willing. "Take your pick," I said. She replied, "Let's start with my stripper pole".

I then stood her in front of it and bent her over, lifted her hands backwards over her head and clasped her wrists around the pole. I handcuff them into place and move to her feet. I place the spreader bar between her feet and locked it into place.

Next, I blindfolded her and put in the ball gag. It was such a sight.

I picked up a short leather whip and began teasing her body with it. I stroked her vagina with it and slid it over her asshole. I felt a slight trembling from her skin as I continued this activity. I then grabbed her cunt and massaged it thoroughly. I got her moist and then I walked around and said to her "You have been a naughty girl" I then give her a light tap of the whip on her ass, then again a little bit harder.

I took the ball gag off and asked her "What do you have to say for yourself you dirty little slut."

"Nothing, punish me" She replied.

"Certainly, you do need punishing" I said.

I then patted the whip on her back and then gave a firm smack to her backside.

"I'm going to give you some more punishment," I said.

I undid her handcuffs and removed the spreader bar. I took off the blindfold and lead her to the sling. I removed her corset to leave her in nothing but shoes. She laid face down suspended in the air with her hands raised and secured in place behind her head. There is now a gimp mask on her head. Her legs are secured and spread far apart.

I picked up some purple candle wax, lit it up, and watched as it began to melt. I began to pour the hot sticky liquid, the first of many she would receive that day, on to her back. She struggled as the hot stuff touched her skin. She then relaxed as I continued to pour more onto her body. It dripped down her sides and she enjoyed it. I then used different colour waxes and she moaned in delight.

Her body now began to resemble a Jackson Pollack painting. All that wax was stinging with heat as it began to cool on her body. She had no boundaries, no inhibitions, and certainly no shame. I undid her restraints and removed her from the sling. I lead her to the wrought iron bars by the window. I removed the gimp mask and then put the ball gag back in her mouth. She had her hands behind her back handcuffed to the iron bars. She had only her high heels and the candle wax adorning her body.

I now removed my coat and lifted her up; she gazed at my cock with the metal cock ring around it. I then moved toward her pussy and slide it in.

I heard a loud moan from her mouth as I slid it all in. I slowly slid it in and out and began to build up rhythm and speed. She continued to moan as I increased my pace. She pulled against her handcuffs as pleasurable lust flowed through her body. Her moans of ecstasy permeated through the gag in her mouth.

The unmistakable sound of metal on metal as the handcuffs encountered the iron bars filled her lounge and it continued for quite some time.

It seemed time to finish her off. I removed the handcuffs, took out the ball gag.

"Take off your gloves and your shoes" I said to her. "Head to the shower" I added.

I then removed the apparatus I was wearing.

She stood there outside the shower waiting for me. It was a large glass enclosed shower. I ushered her inside and pumped away. Feeling her impending orgasm I pushed harder and harder until orgasm shot through her and sent shivers through her spine.

I proceeded to continue my resolve until I was ready to shoot my load. She placed her face in front of my cock and took stream after stream of my hot jizz on her face.

She sat back, caught her breath, and smiled at me. I then stepped back to her and pissed all over her face. "Thank you" she said to me.

I left the bathroom and deconstructed and packed away all the equipment, and got dressed in my suit for activities later that day. As I finished up, I saw her walk out of the bathroom still naked covered in candle wax, cum, and piss. She reached into a cabinet and pulled out an envelope.

She tossed it to me and said, "There is a little extra there for you". There was quite a bit extra in fact.

"Thank you madam, please call again" I replied.

"Oh I certainly will" She said.

Learning to Dance (BDSM)

she learns an important lesson.

As she sat on a sofa in the corner of the crowded club, she wondered for the hundredth time why she let her friends talk her into this. She never thought she'd see the inside of this place again, after....what happened. She recognized faces here and there in the crowd, but drew her solitude around her like a screen and nursed her glass of ice water. She shifted again on the couch, feeling ill at ease and foolish for allowing herself to be goaded into coming out at all. She shifted yet again, crossing and uncrossing her legs as she tried to achieve a more comfortable position. She leaned her head back momentarily as a wave of fatigue washed over her; she closed her eyes and tried to will herself a thousand miles away.

"May I have this dance?" A deep, masculine voice resonated in her ears and cut across the bass beat of the music to startle her out of her musings. She squinted against the flashing lights that backlit the figure standing in front of her, trying to see his face. He stepped closer, his hand outstretched to help her rise from the couch. Not bad, she thought to herself as she got her first good look at him. He was taller than she was, even in the 4-inch stiletto heeled boots she habitually wore when she was at this particular club. Nice build, lean and lithe as an acrobat. Dark hair and dark eyes which were returning her frank assessment with a patient, steady smile. The smile...now, that was very nice. His lips were well-shaped and curved slightly upwards at the corners with a hint of wickedness. A very kissable mouth, she decided.

"I don't believe we have ever been introduced...my name's Master Titus." Her eyes widened slightly; she had heard stories about this Man but had never seen him in her time among the community. His smile widened as he saw her flash of recognition. "And your name is..." he prompted, giving the hand that he was still holding a gentle squeeze in encouragement. She almost blurted her old scene name out, then caught herself in mid-syllable and subsided in embarrassed confusion. "You must have a name little one...or are you too new to have chosen one yet?" She shook her head and tried for a sophisticated, worldly laugh that came out sounding like a high-school giggle. "Well, no matter...you can tell me your name when you're ready. Now, how about that dance you promised me?" He led her, still holding her hand, out into the press of bodies in the middle of the dance floor. There was hardly room to stand, much less dance, but they managed as best they could. As she danced, she let the pulse of the music get inside her and loosen her muscles, so that by the end of the song she had lost all the stiff discomfort from earlier. The next song blared out from the speakers; a new song that was darkly sensuous and that she had wanted to dance to from the first time she heard it.

Suddenly, an over-enthusiastic dancer behind her bumped into her hard and threw her forward into her dancing partner. He caught her before she could trip and fall, and held her steady in strong arms as she regained her footing. The music swirled and beat around them, and he kept his arm around her waist as they both started to move in rhythm again. The nearness and warmth of his body got her flustered and she felt awkward and clumsy. He leaned in and breathed in her ear, "Relax girl, follow my lead...give over control and see where it takes you..." His voice, deep and calm like a mountain lake, washed over her. She closed her eyes and allowed her perception to narrow just a bit, to feel the shift and thrust of his body as he danced and matched her body's movements to his. "That's it, good girl...let go..." His lips brushed against her cheek and she could smell his clean, masculine scent as he pulled her in even closer. The music was building to the crescendo; his other hand came up and ran through her hair before taking a firm grasp of it and suddenly pulling her head back, exposing her neck and making her back arch. She gasped at the speed and the controlled ferocity of his action, and her first reaction was to pull up - to struggle.

He stood stock-still and held her firmly, right there in the middle of the dance floor. Her eyes had flown open and now were locked with his as she tried to read what his motives were for doing this. His dark eyes betrayed nothing, and looked back into hers with the same calm patience that was there when he first asked her to dance. She struggled again, her hands coming up to push against his chest as her neck muscles strained to pull her head fully upright. She wasn't going anywhere; he had her locked in a very firm, very controlled embrace. As awareness of her helplessness sank into her, a strange wave of emotion stirred her to relax again. Her eyes that had been staring so defiantly into his softened and went dreamy; her lips that had been tight and pursed softened and opened slightly to release a low sigh. She relaxed against him, her hands dropping to her sides as she finally hung, almost limp, in his arms.

His eyes gleamed as he smiled at her and released her hair. He leaned in and gave her a swift, hard kiss on the lips before taking both her hands in one of his and leading her off the dance floor and outside to the patio area. The space was deserted and a blessed relief from the heat and noise of the dance floor. He perched on top of a high bar-seat and motioned for her to sit opposite him.

"Now, why don't you tell me who you are, little one." His calm demeanor belied the hint of steel she heard in his voice. She blushed crimson and considered telling him an outright lie. But she considered him, and remembered exactly who he was, and decided to tell the truth. He would definitely walk away, that she had no doubt of, but all she would have wasted was an evening and a dance.

"My name is Elizabeth." Now it was his turn to show recognition; his nose flared a bit and his lips thinned as he breathed in sharply. She hastened to add to the end of her statement, "....Sir." As a veiled challenge, as proof that she had training, she wasn't sure why she dared that. She saw a tiny flash of mirth in his gaze, and his lips curled at the corners again in acknowledgement of her salvo across his bow.

"Well well....I heard that you had left the scene completely. I suppose my information was inaccurate." He studied her as she debated what to say next. A part of her brain was screaming to just thank him for the dance and leave the damn club and never look back. However, to her amazement and shame, she started recounting the whole story of all the mistakes that she had made that led to her self-imposed exile. She was brutally honest with him; the months of telling the story to her friends and all the gossip-seeking hangers-on that had hounded her for juicy tidbits had cut away all the self-serving and pitiful excuses that she had originally made to herself. She took responsibility for her grave errors and gave all the reasons for her subsequent decision.

He was silent for many long moments after she had finished speaking. His gaze was far away as he sat; she could only believe that he was trying to digest what she had just told him. Finally he nodded and said, "Well, you can imagine the different versions of the story that were floating around about that whole thing. First, and correct me if I'm wrong, you had only had one or two experiences before your first private party, right?"

He waited until she nodded before continuing.

"Then it was how long, a week, before a collar was offered?"

Again, he waited until she nodded. He made a low rumbling noise that put her in mind of a male lion gnawing on a gazelle's shin-bone.

"And given the people involved, I imagine that you were played with very hard. I know their styles. I hope you will indulge me, but I want to know how you liked their different approaches..." He leaned forward, putting both his hands palm-down on the small table between them, and looked into her eyes with an eerily intense focus.

She was silent for a minute, letting all the memories swim to the surface of her mind. The only problem with this, she thought, was that I have to re-visit all the good memories as well as the bad. She started to talk. She told him about her real journey into pain, her first endorphin high and what it did to her. She told him about the crushing let-down afterwards that also iimprinted its conditioning on her. She told him about the edge-play, pushing her limits, breaking her limits in some places, and how it helped her completely open her psyche to new realms of possibility. And finally she told him about how she had let her emotions get involved, and how she was the most ashamed of that because it was what had prompted her to commit the cardinal sin of defying her collar to one Dom and secretly seeing another Dom.

He smiled. She sat there silently and was amazed that he was smiling. The man sitting across from her was probably the most well-known traditional Dom in the city, and he was smiling at her after hearing how she made fools of two of his brother Doms in the eyes of the rest of the community. Her incredulity must have shown in her expression because he let out a long, soft chuckle and stood up to move directly in front of her. Looking down into her eyes, he took her face in his hands.

"Elizabeth, I hope you hear this and believe it. I'm sure that you've heard that I don't play with "newbies". There's a reason I don't. The intensity of my style is not suited for people new to the lifestyle, not because they can't handle the pain level but because it takes them places that they have no knowledge of how to deal with. What happened to you, little girl, was a bad case of "first frenzy" that was taken advantage of. It takes probably six months of steady play and teaching for a new sub to finally come to terms with the physical and psychological effects of BDSM;

then and only then are they capable of making a rational choice to be collared to a particular Dom. What you did was wrong, of course...but in my mind there are greatly mitigating circumstances for what happened."

His words and his quiet, calm demeanor eased the last vestiges of hurt and self-loathing in her. Tears formed in her eyes as she gazed up at him; she trembled and started to raise her hands to brush the tears away before he could see them. He beat her to it, raising his thumbs to gently wipe the moisture away then licking each thumb and tasting her tears. That low rumbling came again, a leopard as he savored his kill this time. He seemed to make an internal decision and pulled her off the barstool and into his arms.

Holding her firmly against his chest he murmured, "If you wish, I would like to take you home with me for this one evening." She stiffened in surprise. Never in her wildest thoughts did she think that this would be an even remotely possible outcome of the evening. His smile widened slightly and he added, "After all, I have always been curious about the infamous Elizabeth....I want to see for myself what you're capable of..." She blushed again when she heard that and he laughed out loud. She also recognized his answering salvo in the word "infamous" and the fighter in her rose to the challenge.

Elizabeth nodded her assent and allowed him to lead her back through the club and out the front door. She had ridden with her friends to the club so she didn't have a car of her own; she whispered to one of her friends as she passed where she was going and what she was doing, and was rewarded by a huge gasp and an equally huge "thumbs-up" sign.

In his car during the short drive to his house, they talked about light, inconsequential things - a new movie he'd seen, a new book she'd read. First date material, she thought with an internal chuckle. When he parked and turned the car off in his driveway, the first flutter of nerves hit her stomach. What if....what if she couldn't live up to his standard, what if she panicked and used a safeword before she could really show him what she was capable of....the thoughts swirled in her mind all the way up the walk and through the front door, which he held open for her in an exaggerated show of gallantry. He led her through the house and back into a living room that was decorated in warm earth tones with splashes of vivid colors here and there.

"Relax girl, take those ridiculous heels off before you break your ankle." He smiled his wicked smile to take the sting out of the words. He disappeared back into the darkened house, presumably to get drinks, as she started the process of unlacing, unhooking and unzipping her boots. He came back with two tall glasses full of ice water just as the second boot hit the floor and Elizabeth breathed a deep sigh of relief. He chuckled and handed her a glass, then sat down in a large overstuffed leather chair and put his feet up on an ottoman before taking a large gulp of his water. Silence settled in the room; Elizabeth didn't know what to say, and he was seemingly content to drink his water. She felt his gaze upon her and glanced over, then hastily looked away. His eyes were too intense to hold their gaze for long.

"Stand up." The statement, so quietly spoken, yet rang with command and she obeyed without thinking. "Come here." She slowly walked toward him, stopping at the edge of the ottoman on which his feet rested. He looked at her and raised an eyebrow. Her body reacted instantly; her hands went behind her back to clasp together, her head lowered slightly and she dropped slowly to her knees. My god, she thought, some things you never forget, even if you wanted to. She could feel the same curious narrowing of focus that she had encountered on the dance floor earlier, and the same silken lassitude as when he had held her head back.

"Now, Elizabeth, we can go about this one of two ways. The first way, we can negotiate the evening's scene, from start to finish, then act it out, then I take you home. Nothing will be left to chance or guesswork, and you can feel secure that you will know exactly what will happen. The second way requires a bit more trust on your part...that you hand yourself over to me for the night and let me lead you where I think you want to go. The choice is yours..." He leaned back in his chair and watched her with calm assurance.

She knelt there and thought about the two options. The first one had its merits - she would know exactly what was going to happen and know that she could handle it. But then she realized that what she really wanted was to submit to this man and relinquish that control, at least for a night. She cleared her throat and murmured, "This girl would choose the second option, Sir..." She risked another glance up at him and was rewarded with his smile.

"Well then, little girl, stand up and take your clothes off for me." He sat forward as she stood up and began to slowly unbutton her blouse. Each piece of clothing was removed and folded carefully, and put on the couch behind her. She was meticulous, remembering her former training. Finally, she stood naked before him, her head bowed and hands clasped behind her back.

He stood up and walked to her. Slowly he circled around her, touching and inspecting her body. She could feel his warm fingers as they stroked up her spine to rest at the back of her neck. His other hand came brushing up her belly to lightly cup a breast. She closed her eyes as his thumb grazed across her suddenly erect nipple. She heard him chuckle softly and then murmur, "Your body is certainly responsive to positive stimulation. Now let's see how you respond to..." His voice trailed off as the fingers that had been so lightly and teasingly playing with her breast suddenly pinched down on the nipple. Her eyes flew open at the sudden onslaught of pain; then she breathed in deeply and relaxed into the sensation, letting the feeling course through her body as she had been taught. He stepped in front of her, still holding her nipple painfully tight between thumb and forefinger. His eyes caught hers; his steady gaze became her focus and she poured out the pain she was feeling as offering to his dominance. His gaze warmed as he sensed her surrender to the sensation he was choosing for her, and he slowly relaxed his hold on her breast. She had not moved a muscle during the whole short ordeal and could see that he was very pleased with her performance.

Master Titus pulled a wide band of black cloth from his back pocket and told Elizabeth to close her eyes. She obeyed, and felt the soft cloth wrap around her head to bind her eyes shut. He tied the blindfold snugly at the back of her head, then took both her hands in his and started leading her forward. She relaxed even further into her rapidly narrowing perception as her sense of hearing and touch were exponentially heightened. She could feel every bump and furrow in the carpet she was walking over; she could hear his soft breathing and the swish of his clothing as he led her.

He stopped her and dropped her hands. She stood still; she could hear assorted clinks and rattles as he moved around her. Finally, she felt him lift her wrist to wrap a wide soft leather cuff around it. She shivered. It had been a very long time since she had been bound like this, and it brought back intense memories of her past experiences. He continued, fastening a cuff on her other wrist then on both ankles. She could feel him attach clips to each cuff, then he gently pulled her forward and guided her hands to the smooth wood arms of a St. Andrew's cross. She almost froze when she realized what was about to happen. She had heard of Master Titus's prowess with all manner of floggers, whips and canes, and that he was a bit of a sadist when it came to the giving of pain. But she had made her choice, and was now in his domain for the rest of the night, for good or bad. With that thought, she leaned forward and stretched her arms up to be fastened to the rings.

He secured her to the cross, making sure her feet were firmly planted before attaching the cuffs on her ankles to the bottom rings. When she was secured to the cross, he patted her hip like he was gentling a restive horse and then moved away. She could her him moving around behind her. Then his hand was on her shoulder again, bracing her as he stroked the heavy leather flogger down her back. The soft leather strands felt cool and sensuous on her heated skin and she moaned softly.

"Listen to my voice little one, and relax. Let the sensation flow through you like I know you can. You know your safewords; and you know that I will respect them. But for now...relax..." He stepped back and she shivered at the loss of contact. Then the first warm sting of the flogger hit across her buttocks. The still-rational part of her brain had to admire his skill; he knew just how hard to swing the flogger to get her skin warm and responsive before going further. The thuds of the flogger took on a rhythm that she surrendered to. Up her back, across her shoulders, back down to her bottom and then down the backs of her thighs...the leather strands brought the blood to the surface of her skin and made her nerves sing. Instead of anticipating and tensing before each blow fell, she relaxed and let her head drop forward to rest on the cross. She moaned softly as he started to pick up the tempo; the strokes rained down faster on her flanks and back and she realized he was using a flogger in each hand. She took a moment to think about what other interesting things a man who could use both hands independently of each other could do. The images made her moan louder, just in time to gasp as the floggers started to bite harder into her back.

The harder the blows fell, the higher Elizabeth's consciousness soared. She gave in to the pain and let it flood her with endorphins. Just as she felt like she was reaching some sort of apex the flogging stopped, and she almost cried out to beg for more. But then she felt the tip of a rattan cane trace down her back before hearing the swish and then the impact across her bottom. He alternated light, tapping strokes with broad swats and precision cuts that left no part of her body untouched. The fire was growing inside her with every beat; she was moaning continuously and her tears were streaming from under the blindfold. A series of rapid strokes fell, that went from the bottom of her buttocks to her shoulderblades, and then suddenly he was standing close behind her. His hand came up between her legs to cup her sex, then his thumb slid into her in one fluid motion. He knew just where to push; and she screamed as her orgasm crashed over her like a tidal wave. She was mortified to hear the splatter of her essence on the hardwood floor beneath her. He chuckled and bent forward; she felt his hair brush down her side and then a towel was placed between her feet. All she could do was moan and shiver as he slowly unclipped her arms and legs from the cross.

He gently removed the blindfold and she blinked rapidly as the light returned to her eyes. She was shaking and unsteady; he wrapped an arm around her waist and walked her back over to the large leather chair. He sat down and pulled her down onto his lap as if she was a child; and she almost felt like one as he wrapped her up in his arms. From one side of the chair he pulled a soft fleece afghan up and draped it down over her back, then rocked her slowly as he made those curious rumbling noises in his chest. It was like being cuddled by a tiger; she felt absolutely safe with the added awareness that at any time this man could rip her psyche to shreds. Her eyes closed and she relaxed into his warm embrace, the flood of endorphins still singing through her veins.

A strong hand lifting her chin woke her out of her daze. She opened her eyes to see him smiling down at her before his lips claimed hers in a deep, passionate kiss. She opened herself completely to the kiss and poured her emotions into it, as if she could communicate her submission through her lips to his. He rumbled again and his arms tightened around her body before he shifted her up and off his lap. He eased her down to where she could kneel in front of the chair then stood up and started to slowly remove his clothes. She watched as each piece of clothing fell away, mesmerized by his masculine form. When his pants slipped down to pool at his feet she automatically reached out to help him step out of the legs and then folded the pants carefully before laying them atop her own pile of clothes. Then she took back her position kneeling, her eyes lowered, as her cheeks flamed at the sudden flood of lust that took hold of her. She could feel the heat of his body as he stood close to her - she could smell his male scent and it was driving her to distraction.

His hand shot out and grabbed her hair firmly. He stepped close to her and pulled her face in to press against his groin. He held her thus; she breathed deeply and rubbed her cheek and lips against the hardness that was rapidly growing. Another wave of passion dripped slowly down her thigh as she whimpered, before opening her lips to take him into her mouth. She savored the taste of his flesh. He felt like satin-covered iron in her mouth as she fit her lips and tongue snugly around him before sliding him deeper. She heard his growl of approval and felt him tighten his hold on her hair, then he started slowly moving in and out of her mouth. He pushed in hard and she barely had time to relax her throat muscles before he slid in all the way, pressing her nose into his belly and holding her there for a few heartbeats. Then he pulled away from her and she was left gasping and empty.

He bent and lifted her up and onto her back over the wide ottoman, so that her head was hanging off the far end. She was literally balancing on her back as he firmly pulled her thighs apart and settled himself into the saddle of her hips. She braced herself the best she could, grabbing onto the short legs of the ottoman to get some support. She couldn't see him with her head leaning so far back; but she felt his hands stroke down her body, touching every inch of her with his warm palms. His hardness was pressed up tightly against her sex, and she arched herself against him in a wordless plea. His mouth came down to claim a nipple as his hips shifted and he slowly slid himself inside her. His hands on her hips kept her positioned to his liking as he fit himself deeply in her body and started to rock slowly back and forth. The feeling of fullness was delicious, and Elizabeth found herself wrapping her legs around his waist to pull him in deeper.

Her body was spiralling towards orgasm. She flexed her muscles around him and heard his soft growl as he started to move faster and harder. He lifted her knees and bent her almost double, her feet coming to rest against his shoulders as he ground his pelvis against hers. He shifted once again and the head of his manhood pressed and rubbed against her inner spot and she screamed again as her orgasm flooded her. She could feel her juices gush and flow around their joined bodies as he kept moving in her, keeping the pleasure at a peak. Over and over again, her body convulsed with orgasmic tremors as she rode a wave that seemed to never end. She reached out blindly to grab onto him, her breath coming in great gasps as she struggled to process what was happening to her. She had never felt this kind of intense and prolonged pleasure before, and a tiny part of her brain marvelled at it.

Then, as if in the eye of a hurricane, everything calmed. She felt like she was moving in slow motion as she lifted her head to look up at him. His dark eyes were focused on hers and she could see the same pleasure mirrored in his face. He had lost his calm detachment; now she could see the true intensity that he had held back during the evening. His eyes burned into hers as he growled just one word...."Mine." he said. "Mine." She could feel him grow and get harder inside her, and her body answered by squeezing tighter as another orgasm built. "Mine." His gaze sang to her to join him.

With what little breath she had left she whispered, "Yours."

Their bodies exploded simultaneously. She screamed as her orgasm peaked and seared through her body, and he gasped and then let out a primal roar of release as he flooded her body with his seed. They remained locked together as two sets of breathing returned to normal. Elizabeth's head had fallen back again, and she felt his soft lips against her throat as he kissed her body. He pulled her forward so that they both tumbled onto the floor and took her mouth in a long and passionate kiss. Master Titus propped himself up on one arm and brushed the sweat-dampened hair away from her face, caressing her cheek as he gazed once more into her eyes.

He nodded and rumbled again. "Mine."

"Yours."

And the past for Elizabeth was erased and replaced with a new, clean future.

My Words (Taboo Sex)

I wrote being daring then son caught me... and hubby.

I'm not used to doing anything like this. By which I mean sitting down and writing down my thoughts and feelings. Or, come to that, sitting here naked writing down my thoughts and feelings.

Because that's what I am – naked – and that's why I'm trying to take some deep breaths and focus on the words. I'm experimenting, you see, trying something new and daring. It's 5.30 in the morning here and the rest of the house is asleep – pretty obviously given how I'm dressed and the fact that 'the rest of the house' comprises by husband and my eighteen year old son.

Other than experimenting with something new and daring, it does beg the question of why I would take such a risk and to be honest, I haven't a clue why I'm doing it. I thought it might give me a thrill, sitting here nude with my robe over there in the doorway, every creak of the floors upstairs sending a thrill coursing through my body. And it does – far more than I even dared hope for.

Mike, my husband, will no doubt be asleep until around nine, as this is his day off, but Adam, my son, will need to be up by around half-seven to get himself together enough to get off to college. Okay, so I should be safe enough for another hour or two, but it doesn't change the fact that I am totally naked here and the guys are just a few feet away – vertically – without a clue.

I know from the pillow talk that sometimes gets us purring that Mike would love what I'm doing, and get a real kick out of the risk I'm taking. But Adam? Well there you have it really. He is the risk in so many ways. He's been peeking – or trying to – for a few years now, but if he ever saw me like this, I think he'd explode. Not that I actually want him to. See me that is, or explode for that matter. But just knowing that if a small grenade went off under his bed and he charged downstairs he might just catch me... well, it gives me a little thrill if truth be told.

It's not just the risk, though, that makes this such a thrill. I don't know if you've ever walked around your house naked but it feels so weird and wild. I'm typing this in our living room at the rear of the house and it's dark outside – I can't see if there's anyone out there looking in at this naked lady, sitting typing. I know that the chances of that actually happening are next to zero – the back of the house looks out on a small copse of trees that border a local golf course, and keen or not, very few golfers ever play before it's light – but it still feels so daring, and I feel so exposed.

I have been seen before during daylight hours – twice in the seven years we've lived here, and only ever topless – by golfers whose drives must have been sliced horribly to end up so deep amongst the trees. Not that they were complaining after locating their missing balls and getting a very brief peek at a local half-naked housewife, I imagine – but neither occasion was deliberate. Even though I'm typing this completely naked, take it from me that I'm too shy to deliberately let any passing golfer see anything untoward. I will, however, admit to 'just happening' to be in the kitchen at the front of the house wearing just rather flimsy undies a couple of times when I was fairly sure that a young businessman – a former neighbour – might be wandering past on his way to work. A rough patch in an otherwise happy marriage, or possibly an early sign of latent horniness.

5.50 now and every minute that passes makes me feel ever more exposed and, I have to admit, rather more aroused than I imagined I might be after this amount of time. There's still ages to go before there's any real danger and I'm starting to think that's just as well. The urge to please – pleasure – myself is getting stronger by the second and let's face it, I can do it, can't I? Ooh, I can, it seems – that was a slight pause as I let my hands caress – the right word – my bare breasts and then slide down my belly to a very warm, very wet part of me. I can even call it my pussy out for you since this is now definitely 'me time'.

The typing is becoming a tad disjointed now as playing is taking on a more distinct role. I'm not really fantasising or anything – just being here, being naked and playing with myself is enough. I have sensitive breasts – tits (I do like that word no matter that it's not supposed to be a 'feminine' way of referring to them) – and just cupping their weight in my hands, my thumbs rubbing across my rigid nipples – oh it's such a delight. And leaning back in this little chair, my fingers probing my wetness and heat. That's a form of heaven.

Exposure like this is constantly thrilling me in new and wilder ways. I know my tits have been seen before by those who really shouldn't, but all of me? My pussy? Never. And it's not just that I have nothing on below my waist – any woman can sit with knees touching, naked, and shows nothing really – but I'm constantly leaning back and spreading my thighs, exposing the hot, pink centre of me. I don't want to be caught like this – but I do want to be in danger of being caught like it.

Still only 6.10 (my typing really is slowing down) and I'm just getting hotter and hotter. The floorboards upstairs keep creaking as they settle and warp with the temperature changes, and every noise sends my pulse sky-rocketing. I was tugging gently on a nipple when that last creak came and my fingers tightened involuntarily, and I gasped with the thrill it sent though my naked form. My belly muscles pulsed and brought me ever close to climax.

And here I am, fingering hard and frequently now, suddenly sure that I am going to do something I've never done before in this house: I'm going to bring myself to orgasm with both the guys here in the building, while I sit here naked, trying not to whimper too loudly. I'm having to leave a good thirty seconds or more between every sentence I type and the feeling of pure decadence is growing with every minute. Every nerve ending is tingling, even the breaths that I take are sending shivers of real pleasure through my veins.

I don't reach climax easily – never have – but sitting here in this dark, silent house (give or take a little creak), I just know that it's going to happen soon and it won't matter that I take an age to finish because there's no one to interrupt. It's luxury mixed with liberal doses of daring and thrills. My heart beat is pounding loud and fast, I'm sweating despite wearing absolutely nothing, I'm using a little cushion to muffle the increasingly loud moans that I can't help but make, and the first little bucks and twitches are fluttering deep in my belly.

A double first, this will be – because I know it must be now – the first time I've ever climaxed like this and the first time I've ever thought to write down my thoughts as I get closer and closer. Both of those things are hot on their own, but together... oh what a combination! I almost – almost wish...

Oh god that last creak was very loud...

[this section was edited later to make it legible]

I think I should stop – that wasn't just the house settling – that was a footstep up there.

Bit of a problem and hard to type. Started really shaking. Tried to get up to get robe but belly fluttering like mad...

Another creak and this is trouble...

Oh fuck...

Can I write that? And what the fuck does it matter? I'm too close...

That wasn't just a flutter, it's starting. And that was a definite creak caused by a foot...

Oh my god this can't be happening...

It's from the back of the house. It's Adam...

I thought I had so long. Got to get robe...

Oh dear patience! Can't get up. Can't stop it...

Stairs! Oh my fucking god... that was a spasm... deep...

Oh god he's going to... I can't... oh...

Adam!

[this next section was written six hours later]

What can I say. You must know I didn't mean to be caught. I tried to keep writing because I thought it would stop things. Wrong, I know. Now, at least.

He walked right into the room before he even realised anything was happening. I'd already started – to climax, that is – as you can probably tell from what I managed to write, but when Adam strode into the room just a few feet in front of me I lost all control. His eyes were real early morning until I let out the first moan and then they focused so hard and fast. Focused on my totally bare breasts. And then on my fingers as they rubbed hard and frantically across my exposed pussy. It just made me cum harder and harder, and the harder I was climaxing, the more my boy stared at me. His boxers bulged and that made me cum harder. He whispered 'wow' and that made me cum harder. He put one hand on the front of his boxers – I cum harder. He said 'mum, are you...?' and I started to really wail as I cum yet harder. I tried to apologise even as my hips were bucking, my tits bouncing as I climaxed so close to my own son. So help me I held out my hand towards him – his hands.

He understood what I meant somehow. He grabbed my free hand and squeezed it tightly as his own free hand started to rub furiously at his so obvious erection through his boxers. When I managed to say 'yes' staring at that bulge he misunderstood that. He pushed the boxers down and his young cock sprang into view. Our hands unlocked and I grabbed at him even as his hands landed on my upper chest.

I rolled backwards, still bucking, still climaxing – not a multiple, but the longest orgasm I've ever had – and Adam landed on top of me. I think I tried to say 'no' but his cock parted my already soaking wet pussy lips in a single move.

A single move later, the head of his cock went from parting me to thrusting into me. And then he was there. He looked as surprised as I felt, but momentum won the day. My son, my baby just a couple of decades before, had his rock hard cock inside my soaking wet, hot pussy. My son was fucking me.

The 'no' I'd tried to say before turned to a stream of one word endlessly repeated: 'yes', I bucked and writhed and grabbed at his butt to pull him as deeply inside me as I could. He cum fast and I stopped him pulling out, and then kept him there deep inside me as his cock barely sagged before he was rigid again.

I'd finished my orgasm at one level, but at another I was still in the throes. I told him that I'd never felt so hot, so aroused. I told him I knew that this was all wrong for so many people – but so right for me. I told him that I'd never known before, but knew now. I told him that I adored him in so many ways. I told him to fuck me, hard.

What can I say? We fucked, made love, Words were whispered as eyes tried not to stray towards the ceiling. There was nervousness bordering on fear. There was shock verging on disbelief. There was my son's hot, rigid cock moving with something close to desperation as he repeatedly, blissfully impaled me, thrusting deep and hard.

I started to cum fully again, biting into his shoulder to stifle what would otherwise have been howls of delight. Adam's body took its cue from me and he buried his face in the cushion beside my head and he thrust one more time, deeply, cock twitching as he spurted what felt like a gallon of cum deep inside my pussy.

Time blurred as the moments of climax stretched into infinity and I felt myself almost merging with my boy as our mutual climaxes intertwined and we bucked an shuddered together. I don't care if I never cum that perfectly ever again in my life: that was perfection.

Focus returned after however long it was – minutes, maybe – and we found ourselves entwined, sweat-soaked, panting, gasping, bodies twitching with a series of aftershocks that felt, to me at least, stronger than some full orgasms that I've experienced in the past. In the minutes that followed as our breathing finally began to slow, I held Adam closely to me. At one point he seemed to want to slip away but I shook my head and grasped his slippery back harder. I told him that he was now the perfect son, with no idea where that thought came from. He told me I was beautiful.

It was a distant creaking floorboard that finally had us untangling our limbs and dashing for the few items of clothing that had been discarded at different points earlier. Adam's eyes were wide, a little fearful, almost pleading.

"You've just got down here, okay? Nothing unusual going on, and I asked you whether you wanted a coffee and that's where we are now, got it?" I whispered quickly, running my hands through the tangles of my hair, then louder I added for the benefit of approaching ears, "Not like you to be up this early. Bad dream?"

Adam nodded and looked directly into my eyes, "Totally the opposite, mum. I never wanted it to end."

Just before Mike made his appearance I let my voice drop for one sentence, "It doesn't have to end, got it?"

The look of relief on my boy's face almost sent another aftershock through my belly. I had to clear my throat as my husband yawned his way into the room. "Hey Mike, good morning and do you want a coffee as well since I was making one anyway for the earlybird here?"

Mike yawned again, nodding and muttering 'morning' He waited until Adam turned towards the doorway and wandered through to the dining room, and then Mike patted my butt through the little robe I had pulled on. "Looking hot, honey."

"New exercise regime."

"I meant cute hot, but if that's a result of the new exercises, I'm all for it."

"Oh," I managed, turning towards the kettle so my blush was less obvious, "I think this new routine will work out just fine."

Mike gave a soft chuckle, "I take it you didn't expect Adam to be up so early, then?"

Trying not to panic, I pulled what I hoped was a totally quizzical look and looked back at my husband, "Sorry?"

"I guess you didn't realise it," Mike whispered, lifting a hand to cup my left breast, "but you can see your nips rather well though this robe. No wonder he was looking a bit awkward when I come in here."

I gasped and pushed Mike's hand away, covering my breasts with my arms and glancing at the doorway through which Adam had departed. I replied with a frantic whisper, "I never even gave it a thought, I'm sorry-"

Mike's finger to my lips stopped me short, "It doesn't bother me, angel." He shrugged, a grin playing around his mouth, "In fact it's rather sexy."

"Don't you mean kinky? That's our son through there!" Oscar-quality.

"That's as may be, but he's not a little boy anymore, and that is one damned sexy look." Mike looked deep into my eyes, "I dare you to stay dressed like that and make an excuse to get Adam in here for a while."

I feigned surprise and doubt, but I didn't need to feign the colour rising in my cheeks, "He's still a teenager, just. Doesn't take too much to get guy like him excited and you're really saying..."

Mike kissed my forehead, "Yes I am. I know it's a bit weird and wild but I think it's so hot." He pulled me into a hug and I could feel just how hot it was making him. He was rigid and I swear steam was rising from him.

I muttered, "I don't know..." to give myself a few seconds to try to think. Oh I wanted to do it – in a way to repay Mike for my 'sins' but also, of course, because I just wanted it so badly. But there again, could anything be said that would give the game away about what had already happened? Would-

Mike interrupted me with the saving move, "Look, angel, really... please? I need to go to the bathroom. Promise me you'll think about it real hard because I swear to you if you do this I'll do anything you want in return – absolutely anything." He paused and took a deep breath, "Just knowing he's seen you in that robe will keep me happy for weeks, but that's because I've kinda had a bit of a fantasy thing about this for years, okay? I admit it now because this is as close as it's ever got and I am just so silly desperate for this."

My jaw had dropped but as Mike turned on his heel and was about to take his own embarrassment through to the bathroom, I found myself whispering "Are you really sure?"

I think the look Mike gave as he paused and faced me was the most shocked anyone had looked that wild morning – and possibly also the most excited, and that's really saying something. "Oh angel, I am so sure."

"Give me a minute to think it through."

Mike disappeared at something close to a run and I shot into the dining room to find Adam.

"Did you overhear any of that? Yes? Good. Now listen, you've got to make out you're all-"

"Reluctant, shocked – I know, mum. I've never seen you like that before, it's all a shock, sorry but yes you turn me on..."

"You're smart." I sighed with relief "And just take all your permissions from your dad – ignore anything I say unless it's 'yes', got it"

Adam nodded, "I promise."

I didn't really trust myself to say anything else and in any case needed to take my place in the kitchen for Mike's return. I just smiled, shrugged and ran.

As I waited for my newly-revealed-as-kinky-thankfully husband to return I busied myself with making the drinks. Life can change completely in a matter of seconds, and two separate life-changing incidents had occurred for me within an hour. I made a mental note to by a lottery ticket.

"Well, did you come to a decision?"

Mike's hushed, slightly shaky voice suddenly close behind me gave me a start. So much so that I didn't think before coming out with a very flippant and totally unplanned "What's it worth?"

"Like I said," Mike's voice was even less steady, "anything at all. A hundred orgasms at your favourite hundred places, stripping for your book club, walking across molten lava..."

"How about I reserve the right to never mention any of this again and just say 'no' next time you refer to it or ask?"

"That was always a given for me, so of course that's agreed."

I gave a half-smile, "That was the right answer, buddy. Anything else would have made me wonder some more." After which I would have agreed anyway, but Mike wasn't to know that, "Although I might just add that I want you to organise a trip to some exotic club or something like that."

"You got that, too – and anything else you might think of..." My husband paused and strove to calm himself, "you're really sure that-"

I held up my hand, then once I was given some silence, loosened the tie on my robe, "I'm thinking you haven't really figured this all through, right? I mean, are you expecting a little direct view or just through my robe?"

"You'd really let him see for real?"

"Stop dribbling. I figure if we're going for a show then it should be done well enough to please the principal audience – you."

Mike visibly swallowed, "Oh jeez, baby, I would love that. And I'll make it up to you a thousand times over."

"Make it ten thousand times and maybe, just maybe I could consider a tad more than a peek... Or would that be too much to-"

It was Mike's turn to interrupt me as he grabbed me and kissed hard. He broke away after a few seconds and whispered "Not too much, no definitely not, and look... baby, I won't ever think bad of you for being so wild, so giving, no, just the opposite, but if we don't get this started I might just explode so if you really, really are sure then let's do it, okay?"

I nodded, uncertain of how much my voice would shake if I tried to say anything. And when I smiled, Mike picked up the coffee pot and shakily poured a mugful. He handed it to me and his eyes flicked towards the door. I gave another nod and took a deep breath before taking the first metaphorical steps towards a brave new world. I took a deep breath and swallowed. "Adam? There's a fresh coffee here for you!"

To his credit, Adam managed to stretch the time between my voice calling out and his appearance in the kitchen doorway to almost five seconds. That was an act, but I think the jaw-dropping stare he gave when his eyes took in just how much I was showing through that flimsy robe was all too genuine. Mike later said it was this single most thrilling moment of his life – up to that point – and I can believe it to judge by what I felt at that same second. I know all that had gone on before – and so very soon before, at that – but this was different in a million ways. Not least of which was the fact that there was some sort of tacit approval of mine and Adam's kinkiness.

The tacit approver cleared his throat, "Well come on in and grab it, then. You mum's gone to a lot of trouble to get it ready for you."

I couldn't help but give a soft chuckle when Adam started to look confused as well as shocked, "The coffee, I think your dad means."

"Oh, er, yes, right, coffee."

I raised an eyebrow when he didn't move, "Something wrong?"

"No! I mean... er... nothing at all. No, sir, nothing wrong in the slightest, nothing.... Mum?"

"Yes, angel?"

"Do you... I mean did you... you do realise your, um, that thing you've got on... well – and this is like to both of you – well, it's very... that is, it's not very... very thick, is it? Mum? Dad?"

Mike looked down over my shoulder, his fingers now gripping my shoulder almost painfully tightly, "It does seem a little bit revealing. Still not to worry, huh? It's not like it's a bad view."

I looked down myself and shrugged, "Nice of you to say so but if it offends in any way, Adam, I'll pop upstairs and slip into something more-"

"No! I mean, no, it's, er , fine by me, ha, ha. That is if you – both of you – actually realise what... that is, how it's kinda making me, er, feel..."

"Well I know how it's making me feel," Mike managed, "And I sure don't mind you getting an idea of why I think your mum is and always has been so vey sexy."

I tapped his hand, "You're making me blush."

"No," Mike said, his voice thick, "This is what might make you blush." Without warning, he brought his other hand to my other shoulder. Both hands gripped the flimsy robe and pulled it apart, baring my breasts before I could so much as squeal, "Aren't I the luckiest guy in the world?"

Adam's eyes were on stalks – and there seemed to be another one in his shorts, "No, luckiest guy ever has got to be me. I just gotta say it mum, dad... wow!"

"Guys!" My protest – if that's what it really was – sounded weak even to my own ears, "This is not my style. I'm no show off as you well know-"

Mike kissed my neck, "Well you should be. Right, son?"

He took a step closer, almost within touching distance, "You are so gorgeous, mum, really. I've never seen anyone so... well.... sexy."

"Everything about your mum is sexy," Mike was almost panting, "She even feels sexy...

One of his hands cupped a breast and I gasped – but barely flinched, "Isn't this a little..bit much now?"

Mike shook his head, his hand squeezing just a little more firmly, "All part of the whole sexy experience..."

Adam was visibly trembling, "Dad... mum might be right because... I'm finding it hard not to try to find out just what that whole sexy experience feels like..."

I didn't trust myself to say a word, but when Mike said, "I wouldn't blame you for finding out" I gave a shuddering whimper.

Although Adam had just been given his dad's blessing, he still sought out my gaze, looking for the ultimate permission. I managed to scream 'yes' with my eyes even as I whispered the verbal equivalent.

Despite what had happened just an hour earlier, there was something approaching desperation in how Adam's hands sought my nakedness. He cupped both breasts in a single, swift motion, his eyes almost rolling back into his skull as he squeezed with infinite gentleness. My nipples, already hard, pressed deeply into the flesh of his – my son's – palms and I did nothing to disguise the moan that pulsed from me. I was dimly aware of Mike caressing my hair, his hands trembling.

Without any idea of how it come to pass, I found myself upright with my son's lips caressing my tingling, rigid nipples. Mike's hands moved to my neck, arched back and starting to gently perspire. My robe fluttered open, baring my sex, as we moved in staggers and shudders from kitchen to the living room, hard stone floor to the depths of the deep, soft pile of a carpet.

My shoulders bore my weight briefly as I sank to the floor, my robe being pulled up and away from my arms, leaving me naked and so totally exposed. Adam's lips had barely broken contact with one or other breast and now that I settled myself there I drew his weight on top of me, almost oblivious to my husband, now kneeling to my left.

Hunger rose higher and higher within me, and I grabbed for the waistband of my son's shorts, my fingers scrabbling for purchase as I began to push them lower, so eager to free the hardness that I felt now against my thigh.

From my side, I heard Mike's voice, questioning, "Honey? I think that's maybe a little too far, yes?"

Adam started to break away for a moment, but my hands, now on his naked butt, stilled him with a squeeze. I sought and made eye contact before answering Mike. "No," I said to him, "it's not nearly far enough."

My son gave a nearly strangled grunt of acknowledgement and roughly pushed his shorts the rest of the way down. It was the matter of just one moment before his now naked torso was once more on top of mine and my legs scissored open.

"Honey? I think you should stop now. Honey?"

"Adam," I said quietly, despite the wild fire within me, "Please, angel... please make love to me."

I felt rather than saw Mike's hand pull at my son's shoulder but Adam batted the hand away, even as he started to say 'yes' over and over.

My husband's voice rose to a shout as Adam thrust the head and heat of his rigid member at my oh-so willing pussy, and my own very different shout welcomed him inside me.

"Adam!" Mike was almost screaming, "Just you stop that right this second!"

"No!" Two voices yelled in unison before one started an ecstatic mantra:

"Oh, angel, you feel so good inside you mother, making love to her... fucking her, yeah? So good, angel, so very, very good."

Adam was already pounding hard at me, all the while pushing his father's hands from off of his sweat-streaked shoulders, his own mantra of grunts and delighted cries accompanying each thrust.

As my son's excitement grew and my husbands despair mounted, I was carried higher and higher on a current of sheer bliss. From somewhere deep within my barely registering consciousness I managed to grasp one important need. "Come in me, angel, come in mum just as hard as you can."

To the background of a despairing wail from his father, Adam thrust as deep as I can remember ever being impaled before spurting his hot, sweet juices far inside me, his one word cry of "Mum!" triggering my own shuddering, wailing climax.

The world was full of stars, my ears ringing, my heart hammering, my focus zeroed in to the heat and hardness of my son's cock as it twitched and spurted deep inside my pussy. I wanted every last drop of him, and I wanted him to know that this was just the start. I wanted Mike to see it and know it as well. As I climaxed, shuddering, with my son, my husband, his father, staring down aghast, I was changed completely and fully. Control, of all and everything, was now mine.

I was still naked an hour later when I found Mike in our old bedroom, staring at the floor.

I sat beside him and patted him on the thigh. "It's not over," I told him, "but you can't count yourself as the number one anymore, understand?"

"That title goes to Adam now, does it?"

I shook my head, "Oh, no. That title goes to me now. Adam was just the first of a new breed for me."

"I don't understand, do you mean-"

"I mean," I interrupted with a laugh, "that I just realised that all the rules, all the little moral compass points... they're all a nonsense when all is said and done. It's time the rulebook got burnt and I will always, always, be grateful to you for supplying the matches." I gave another laugh as his shoulders slumped, "And hey, cheer up because if you have any bright – or indeed, dark and dirty – ideas, just remember I might be willing to try them out. And you might be there when it happens. Fancy a night out down at that strip joint over on Essex Street later?"

It took him twenty seconds before he registered my final suggestion and a quizzical look came into his eyes. "Are you suggesting that we could-"

"That you could maybe take your property along there, you mean?" I raised my eyebrows, "Well now, that was such a dirty little idea you used to try to get me to play along with, but maybe the new me will even be happy to try it out for real. So how about it tonight, cuck?"

"Cuck? Oh... right... I'm not going to enjoy all of this am I? But I'm not so dumb I won't say yes to this sort of suggestion."

"Honey, you may not even know about half of it let along enjoy it. But when you do, I think you're going to become a real fan."

Mike nodded at length, "Maybe you're right at that. Er, you have any intention of... er... getting it on with our Adam again?"

"I've always said that you being a fast learner is one of the things I adore about you. So it looks like I'll have to fuck our boy again then, yeah?"

It was a full thirty seconds before Mike drew a deep breath in through his nose. And then said "Yes, please".

Anal at Last (Anal Sex)

An accountant and his wife enjoy hot anal sex.

To the outside world Dave Blackwood looked like a conservative forty five year old accountant with a nice house two little kids a station wagon and a pretty wife. But to his wife Jackie he was the best sex she'd ever had.

Jackie wasn't entirely surprised late one evening after the dishwasher was packed and the kids securely in bed when her husband asked her if she would like to try 'back door' sex. They had been married for over ten years and had experimented with almost every part of each other's body. The occasional 'rimming' of either of their arse holes had always increased the intensity of their orgasms, but they had never taken the final plunge (so to speak).

"Well, I don't know, Dave. I mean, it feels okay when you lick my bum hole, or stick a finger in a little bit, but you are so big! I ... I think it might hurt too much."

"C'mon, Jackie. It won't be bad. I won't hurt you." He promised.

"I dunno. I'll think about it."

"Okay. You think while I do this." He replied as he pulled her towards him and kissed her. His tongue seemed to travel halfway down her throat, filling her mouth with the soft, rough texture. Jackie's' own tongue found its way into Dave's mouth and the two exchanged explorations of the familiar orifices.

Jackie felt Dave's fingers slipping under her short top to find her swollen nipples. He pinched them softly, making her moan. Her hands were not idle, quickly finding his growing erection hidden in his navy work pants. He pulled his waist away from them, allowing Jackie to open the pants reach inside his red underpants and free his swelling cock.

A little over six and a half inches long and almost two inches wide, Dave had a nice dick. Jackie loved to feel the soft/hard flesh in her hand, in her mouth, and especially in her tight little pussy. The boyfriend she had had before she met Dave wasn't circumcised and had real hygiene problems. She had refused to put his funky knob in her mouth because it smelled so repulsive. It was because of this guy that Jackie vowed to never again fuck a guy who retained his foreskin. Thankfully, Dave had no such issues. His cock was cut and beautifully clean. Her favourite part was his thick brown pubic hair. Even though his head was completely bald the hair of his groin was a lush thick forest. She hated men who trimmed or shaved their pubes. What was the point? She liked a man to look and smells like a real man.

Thinking about being impaled by her husband's dick made her start creaming. She was getting so wet between her thighs; her pants had a growing dark spot below her mound.

Dave felt the cool air on his swollen cock, followed by Jackie's soft touch. Her small fingers barely circled the thick, throbbing flesh. The warmth of arousal flushed through Dave, as he knew what her next move would be. As he had thought, she broke the long kiss and moved her body so that her head was in Dave's lap. Her mouth was a fraction of an inch away from the hot purple head of his prick. She could smell his musk scent, a combination of man smell, sweat, and the heat of arousal.

Jackie's tongue darted out of her mouth to capture the gleaming drop of clear pre-cum from the tiny hole, her lips were soft and puffy, and felt oiled and slippery sliding Dave's cock in and out, twisting it, twirling it. Licking the underside (a major personal favourite), then swallowing it whole again. She sucked first one then the other hairy ball into her mouth and bumped them around, then rapidly swallowed his cock once again. She thought more about Dave's request to try anal sex. They had fooled around 'back there' in bed and in the shower.

A sudden thrust of his hips brought Jackie back to here-and-now. The swollen head pushed up into her mouth, and she instinctively opened wider and bobbed her head down to begin swallowing Dave's penis. Her pussy tightened and she felt the butterflies in her belly as the hot flesh slipped past her tongue and began to enter her throat. She swallowed rapidly to avoid gagging, and once more succeeded in taking that beautiful cock all the way down her throat.

Dave felt her throat contract, and then loosen up as the tip of his cock hit the back of her mouth. The tight, warm feeling that followed as her throat gripped his full length made him groan. He held her head lightly, letting her concentrate on what she was doing, rather than holding up her head. He never understood how she could do it, but even with her mouth full of him, she still managed to swab around the base of his penis with her tongue.

Jackie's lips were touching the soft hair on Dave's belly and her fingers cradled the heavy balls that hung loosely below her prize. She drew back and gripped his length with her fingers, then plunged back down. She began to work loose her own pants, just enough to slip her hand inside. She thrust two fingers into her wet pussy, coating them with her warm sticky juice. Then, she fondled Dave's balls and the tender spot just between them and his butt hole.

Once more she thought about anal penetration. Without thinking, she lubed his ass with her fingers and slid them in quickly, just as she took his cock to the hilt and swallowed hard. Dave's reaction was instant, and surprising. She felt his sphincter tighten at first, then loosen up rapidly to admit her probing fingers, it felt surprisingly like her vaginal canal, Jackie thought. Soft, velvety, wrinkled flesh, moist and warm around her fingers. She felt the small, hard bulge of his prostate gland and rolled it with her fingers. She felt the small organ pulse, and the muscles around her fingers tighten in rhythmic pulses, as the penis in her mouth swelled and pushed out the thick, hot fluid from his belly into her mouth.

She had not remembered getting that much cum so quickly. It poured out of Dave, and filled her throat, jet after hot jet of the salty cream, straight into her stomach. His ass was still clenching her fingers as the spasm subsided. Dave was lying back in the chair, groaning and panting. His whole body was trembling through the release. Slowly removing her fingers from the back, and her mouth from the front, she crawled up next to him and kissed his mouth. Her own mouth held the last drops of his cum, which she pushed into his mouth with her tongue.

"Holy Shit! Jackie! What did you do? OMG! That was intense!" Dave finally gasped out.

"I was just... you know .. Down there and I started thinking about what you said.... and ... um well .... I just wet my fingers and stuck them in." She looked into his eyes for a reaction. "It .... it was okay, wasn't it?"

"Oh, yeah! ... It was REAL okay!"

Dave started to remove the rest of Jackie's clothes, and soon they were totally naked. Jackie's body wasn't as thin as it used to be but she was still really hot. She had small b-cup breasts with tight little nipples that grew quite long when she was aroused. A long torso and thin waist, a slight bulge in her lower belly, and the soft mound between her tight thighs was a smooth, puffy little slit. It was truly all Dave could do to keep from diving into that sweet treasure every time he saw it.

Jackie sidled up to Dave and rubbed her naked body against his. Her mouth found his and the kissing got hotter and hotter. Hands roamed over backs and butts, between thighs and genitals. Dave's fingers slipped into her wet pussy and pulled out soaking wet with her aroused nectar. He rubbed around the tight puckered opening of Jackie's bum hole. She jumped away at first touch, but Dave's soothing voice and soft touch let her relax and enjoy the stimulation.

Jackie felt her bum hole give way, and loosen up as Dave fingered her in small circles. The pressure he exerted grew with each passing moment, until the tip of one finger pushed inside Jackie's back door. She instinctively tightened her muscles, trapping his finger where it was.

"It's okay, Jackie. Relax. I promise it will be alright."

"But ... but ... what if it ... you know ... starts to hurt?" she asked with a worried whine.

"It may feel a little different, but we won't let it hurt. We must do this very slowly, and with a lot of lubrication. Don't worry, when you are ready, you will know it." Dave appeased her.

He continued to transfer her natural lubrication from her vagina to her bum hole, until the point that he was penetrating past her sphincter. He did not want to exchange the bacteria that lived in her colon to her vagina. That could be very bad for her health. As it was, Jackie was curled up with her knees up against her chest, one leg very high and spread wide. Dave had Jackie roll on to her knees with her butt high in the air. He spread her cheeks apart and admired the little star of her arse entrance. He also noticed that her pussy was dripping with nectar. He scooped up the excess that ran down her thighs and applied the slick fluid to her bum hole. He saw the tender opening begin to dilate as her touched the outer rim.

Jackie heard herself moan softly as Dave manipulated her anal orifice. It was as though it was happening to someone else, but she was feeling it all. Her belly was on fire, the heat of arousal coursed through her whole body. Every place he touched jumped with electric tingles. She felt his warm breath at the division of her thighs, and his extended tongue lightly touch her wet vulva. She rolled her hips back to encourage his oral attentions, and opened her arse even wider.

Dave tasted her sweet pussy, then targeted the little bulls-eye just above it. His stiffened tongue slid into her relaxed anal passage, but only a little. He continued to press the tip against the resistance of her virgin hole. He thought of how he relaxed his own bum hole to accept Jackie's fingers earlier. He stopped kissing on her bum hole, and gently slid his first finger where his tongue had been.

"Push a little, Jackie. Push from the inside ... like ... um ... like you do when you have a bowel movement." He explained.

"What if I .... it might .... OH! I don't know if I can!" Came her worried reply.

"Don't push hard, just a little bit to open the inner muscles that usually keep things in. We want them to let something in from the outside, but they work the same way." He maintained the steady pressure with his slippery finger, and reached around her slim waist to press on her tummy. He felt the tightness begin, just below her navel, then the loosening of the tight back entrance as his finger easily slid in to the second knuckle.

"OHHHH! Dave! It ..it went in so easy!" Jackie gasped. "That doesn't hurt at all!"

He worked the finger around in circles, stretching her back door before he added the second finger. This time Jackie pushed as she felt the extra pressure, and instantly received the gratifying fullness. She pushed back against Dave's hand and moaned.

"OH, yes, Dave. That does feel good."

He pulled out his fingers and replaced them with his tongue, again. This time, he was able to fully insert his tongue the way he did when kissing on her pussy. The rich, earthy aroma and taste was different than the front, although he could still smell her nectar rich vulva as well. He managed to introduce a large quantity of saliva into the beginning of Jackie's colon. He once more traded his tongue for fingers, but added a third this time.

Jackie's groans and gyrations increased as the three fingers slowly pushed her bum hole wider and suppler. She pushed steadily with her belly muscles and the sudden release of her sphincter practically sucked Dave's fingers in. She was actually bucking back against Dave's hand, fucking her own butt on the wet fingers.

"Dave! Oh, Dave! It ... it..Ohmigod .. It feels so different!" She panted. "Do it more! OH, Dave, yessssss." She gasped as she thrust very hard and took all his fingers to the palm.

Dave had prepared some additional lubricant, but wasn't sure it would be needed. He pulled Jackie up by the chest, and pressed her back against his chest. He kissed her neck and nipped her ears, his hands gripping her tiny breasts and pinching her nipples. She turned quickly and faced him, knocking him backward on the couch. She kissed him hot and tried to get his penis into her pussy.

"Slow down, Jackie! We have plenty of time." He cautioned her.

"I'm so horny! I want your cock in me! I want to feel you inside me! OH! Dave! FUCK ME!" She cried out.

Jackie raised up on her knees and took Dave's penis in hand. No sooner than the tip grazed the swollen opening, she let herself fall straight down on it. She was so wet and excited; her vagina accepted the entire throbbing penis easily. Her belly slapped Dave's as she impaled herself fully.

"Ohmigod! Yes! OHHHHH, do it ... do me.... Ohhhh! Fuuuuckkk Mmmmmeeee!" She wailed as her body rocked and swayed on the stiff pole. Her engorged clitoris rubbed hard on his belly and she started cumming very soon.

"C ...C.... Cuummmminnngggg!" She announced, breathlessly. Her body shook and her eyes went back in her head. Her mouth was open, but silent with the intense orgasm. She felt her belly roll and tighten, her vagina clamped tightly around Dave's penis in rhythmic contractions. Several final thrusts of her hips ended the cum, "UH..UH ..OHHH!" she grunted and collapsed on Dave's chest.

Jackie had never cum that fast with him. Dave was surprised that she had released so quickly. He barely felt her hot labia on his cock head when her mound slid forcefully against his lower belly. He enjoyed the warm, wet glove of her pussy gripping his shaft. No sooner did he think that, her vaginal muscles drew tight and he felt the gush of her girl-cum flooding his groin.

He felt her heart racing, pounding through her chest to his. Her breathing was ragged and hoarse. She whispered at him, "Oh Dave, so good. Ohmigod, so fine!"

As she recovered from her vaginal penetration, Dave worked his hand around her butt and started massaging her bum hole once more. She purred and thrust her butt upwards, inviting him to continue. Her cum soaked her whole slit, all the way to her bum hole. He used her natural lube to aid in the invasion of her back door. Her body started the lover's dance, her hips rolling, pulling his fingers into her colon.

"Mmm. Yes, Dave! ... I. I want you there. I want your hard cock in my ass!" She blurted out. She kissed him deep and hot, repeating her request.

"Are you sure?" he asked in return.

"Uh-huh. I ... I'm ready, now."

Dave moved her off of him and they got on the soft carpet floor. Jackie was on her back, and Dave placed her knees up high against her chest. Her feet were almost touching the floor near her head. Her vulva and anal opening were spread wide and available. Her nectar coated all of her swollen, red slit. The labia were puffed and open, like butterfly wings.

Dave knelt between her thighs and pulled her body on to his thighs. His erection pointed upwards in front of the glistening treasure box. Jackie pressed it against her slit and rubbed her juices all over it and Dave took a few short strokes in her vagina, before placing his thick, hot penis near the virgin hole.

He pushed the swollen head against the small star and watched it begin to open. The head popped in and Jackie gasped. Dave continued to push, and Jackie's eyes widened.

"Are you okay?" He asked.

She was biting her lower lip, and merely nodded. She had put a few small toys back there; her favorite was a thin vibrator about three inches long. Never could she remember anything this big near her bum hole. She started having second thoughts as she listened to Dave tell her to relax, get used to the feeling. She remembered to push down, and combined with the steady pressing of Dave's penis, her colon suddenly opened.

She felt the ripples of his hard organ passing the tight opening, filling her back door with hot flesh. Before she realised it, she felt Dave's belly against her vulva, and the most incredible fullness she had ever experienced. It felt as though she had to "go", but the surrounding pressure and sensations made it different. She heard herself groan.

"Jackie! Are you all right?" Dave asked.

"Don't move." She replied. "I'm so full!.. It ...it's so strange! It doesn't hurt, but there is a lot of pressure back there."

Dave smiled and tried to think of anything else, because the tightness and heat of her colon was causing his own inner heat to build, very fast. It had been a long time since he had done anal sex with a girl. Most looked at his massive penis and simply refused to try. Jackie" body had accepted him smoothly and without pain. Their foreplay and earlier intercourse had relaxed and lubricated her just fine. This was the way it should be.

Unconsciously, Dave started moving slowly, pulling about halfway out. Jackie grabbed at his hips, "NO! Don't pull out!"

"It's okay! Just relax and when you feel me push, you do the same, inside."

The slow rhythm took a while to syncronise, but soon they were 'Back door dancing' as though they had done it many times before. Dave could not stand much of the new sensations, though.

"Jackie! I'm ... I. OHGOD! .... I can't.... OHHH gonnacummmm!" He cried out, and instantly filled Jackie's arse with his hot seed. He thrust deep into her and emptied his essence into her dark tunnel. The pulsing, throbbing penis spread her wide, and filled her to what seemed to be her belly.

She felt him thicken, and get longer at the same time he called out his fears. She wanted this delicious feeling to go on, but knew she could not stop his cum. The sudden release surprised her, and she felt his hot seed wash her colon in thick, pulsing jets. This first time of receiving something in her bum was truly amazing. Not just the full feeling, but the pressure it placed elsewhere in her belly, the sensitivity of her genitals and the surprising heat of his fluid. It seemed hotter than when he filled her vagina.

About the time she thought he would have to pull out, she felt him touch her exposed clitoris and penetrate her vagina with some fingers. Her body went crazy! Her clitoris exploded, her vagina contracted, and she could feel her bum hole clamping the semi-rigid cock still lodged back there. The same contractions she had felt in Dave's bum hole, earlier were right there in hers! So intense, she cried out her second cum of the past few minutes, humping her body up to meet Dave's. So intense were her movements, that she did, indeed dislodge Dave from the back door. She lay panting, her legs splayed, and cum running from both holes on to the carpet.

Hot Ride (MILF)

It's hard to be invisible when you drive a muscle car.

*****

Chapter I

I was having the day from hell. Nothing was going right and now I needed to drive to our west suburban distribution center to pick up a load of brochures for an upcoming trade show. I grabbed one of the mail room clerks, Kevin, a twenty something young man who was more strong back then brain, and a company van and set off.

Fifteen minutes later we were sitting at a stop light when my helper said, "Whoa, like that is one hot ride." I turned my head to the left and saw a fire truck red Mustang GT convertible sitting at the light. I immediately recognized the beautiful blonde driver; it was my wife Connie. When the light changed to green she nailed the gas and the car rumbled across the intersection.

What the hell was she doing around here? I thought as I cranked a right-turn-on-red and began to follow her. Since I was in an nondescript white delivery van I wasn't worried about being recognized and kept close behind.

"Does your phone have a camera?

"Sure Mr. Keller. Like they all do."

"Good. I want you to film everything that blonde does. Just make sure she doesn't see you."

About a mile later the ragtop pulled into The Paradise Motor Inn, a down on the heels motel. It was a true vestige from the 1950's with a balcony running the full length of the second floor. Connie pulled in and stopped at a sliding window before driving all the way to the end of the building. She parked next to a silver Lexus.

Get out and shoot some close ups...but don't get caught."

Kevin hopped out and I pulled the van into the strip shopping center next door. I parked in their rear lot alongside the garbage dumpsters .

I noticed Connie was wearing the same conservative gray business suit she had on this morning except the black blouse was unbuttoned showing off a lot of cleavage.

Connie was putting the top up when a man in a sport coat snuck up behind her. He spun her around and began kissing her like they were anxious lovers desperate for a rematch.

I had to do something. A stupid idea popped into my head. It would be interesting to hear her response if I invited her to lunch I took out my cell phone and punched her number. I could hear its distinctive ring across the lot. Connie checked caller ID and held her index finger up to her lips shushing her paramour.

She didn't even say hello, "This is a bad time. I'm in a very important meeting add I'll call you this afternoon." She hung up before I could even say my last good bye and resumed kissing her Lothario.

Something snapped. I lost my mind...hate consumed every cell of my body. My soul cried out for vengeance. Divorce was too good, only their deaths would grant me peace. I decided I was going to run them down with the van. I backed out of the parking space to where I had a clear shot at the miscreants. As I lined up to crush them against the side of the Ford a woman with two children walked out of a first floor room and began loading a car trunk only a couple of spaces away. "Damn!" I cursed as I pounded on the steering wheel until my hands ached. I couldn't kill them in front of little kids.

When the enormity I was going to commit a double murder sank in I began to sob. I watched the adulterers walk hand-in-hand up the stairs to their illicit lair; I wanted to confront them but was unable to make my legs move. I was a beaten man. A minute later their door slammed shut, with a do not disturb placard hanging on the doorknob.

Just when I felt my lowest God tossed me a bone. My hand brushed my pocket and I realized I had a set of keys for the Mustang. I immediately knew what I was going to do.

Kevin climbed in the van and said, "Got it boss. I was even close enough to pick up what they were saying." He looked at me and asked, "Hey, like this is real bad, ain't it?"

I managed to say, "Yes Kevin, this is real bad. But you're going to help me change the dynamic."

"Okay, whatever that means. You're the boss."

"Good, I want you to take the van and follow me. I'll be in the hot ride. We'll make a stop before our pickup then head back to the office. You have to promise you will not breathe one word of this to anyone."

"Don't sweat it, I'm cool."

I didn't want the tuned exhaust to alert my wife so I shifted the car into neutral and pushed it into the shopping center's lot before starting it."

My mind was racing. I couldn't believe it...I thought we had a great marriage. The truth had punched me in the face; my wife was a common whore. Tears flowed as I tried to pay attention to my driving. I called a trusted friend who owned a small farm outside of town; more important it had a big pole barn. "Randy, Jim I need a favor and I can't explain why."

Twenty minutes later the hot ride was safely hidden under a tarp in the barn.

When we got back to the office Kevin downloaded his video to my laptop then burned a half dozen extra copies.

I slipped him a $50 and said "Thanks."

"Thanks man. Anything you need you know where to find me."

Then I went down stairs to see our IT guy. "Brian, I have a problem and I hope you can help me. I have a license plate and I need to know everything about the owner ASAP."

"Mr. Keller, we don't usually do stuff like that. I mean it's sort of illegal. But Kevin called and said you were cool."

Fifteen minutes later Brian was standing in my office with a shit eating grin on his face. "I called a friend at the DMV who ran the plates. After that it was easy. This guy's wife posts everything on facebook." He handed me a complete dossier on Alan McAree, adulterer.

Too bad for McAree, I also had his wife's e-mail address and phone number.

It wasn't easy finding an attorney who would draft divorce papers in a couple of hours but find one I did. It cost double his standard $300/hour fee to put together a respectable Petition for Dissolution or Marriage but it was worth it. The saddest thing was to reflect on five years of marriage and realize without any kids and a house mortgaged to the hilt there wasn't a heck of a lot to fight over. Mostly used furniture.

We live in a no-fault divorce state however I refused to back down on the grounds; adultery. We even added a couple of pictures, one of them kissing and the second of them walking into the hotel room. Damn Kevin wasn't bragging when he said he got close.

I had two copies stamped by the Clerk of the Circuit Court in my hands by 4PM. Her affair with McAree was now part of the public record.

I was useless at work so I passed the time cancelling our credit cards and joint checking and savings accounts like my attorney told me to do.

Chapter II

Around that same time the adulterers walked out on the balcony, no doubt tired but basking in the glow of five hours of illicit sex. They walked hand-in-hand down to the parking lot smiling like they didn't have a care in the world. That changed in an instant. There was nothing parked next to McAree's Lexus.

Connie's eyes got big as she searched the parking lot before screaming, "My cars been stolen!" Followed by a chorus of "This can't be happening to me!"

"If we call the police they're going to want to know why you were parked in a hotel lot."

"Shit!" The two of them brainstormed. McAree came up with a plan. "We have to go to a busy restaurant, one with lots of cars. Then you call the police and say it was stolen while you were eating lunch. And I know just the place. It's always blown out. "

McAree drove them to a restaurant about five miles away. "Shit!" Unfortunately neither counted on the lull between the lunch rush and the dinner crowd; there were only a hand full of cars in the lot.

"It's too late to find anywhere else and I've got to get back to work. Just tell the police you had lunch and left your car here to go shopping at the mall or something. I'll be back as soon as I can."

He tried to kiss her but she pulled away. Connie was not happy lover boy was abandoning her to face the cops alone. Her hands were shaking as she dialed 9-1-1.

Ten minutes later a squad car arrived to take her report.

As I did every night I called Connie when I got home however tonight's call went straight to voice mail. I left a friendly message, no sense tipping my hand, "Hi honey, let me know if you'll be on time for dinner." She did not return the call.

I called again at 5:30 and left a message saying to call me so I knew how to time dinner.

By six I was getting pretty pissed off and called again. Connie actually answered. "Oh Jim, someone stole my beautiful car from a restaurant parking lot," she sobbed.

"Where are you? I'll be right over."

"No!" She actually yelled no! "The police are here and I'm handling it." She was in a panic.

"Where are you so I can at least rescue you."

"The officer wants to talk to me. I've got to go." She hung up on me for the second time today.

So I ate my dinner alone; the silence was only broken when I imagined the look on her whoring face when she saw her pride and joy was missing. I'll bet that knocked the post-orgasmic haze off her mind. That was when I laughed.

Around seven a silver Lexus at the end of the block. It made a three point turn in a driveway then stopped. I saw Connie get out and begin the long walk home as he sped away. As she got closer I could see her blouse was buttoned all the way to the collar. She didn't notice me standing on the front porch until she was a couple of doors away.

"Why didn't your boyfriend drop you off in front of the house?"

"Boyfriend," she panicked. "No, don't be silly. No, he's someone I know from work: I think he's one of the sales reps," she stammered.

"So why didn't he drop you off at home so I could properly thank him."

Connie began babbling something about him being late for something and not able to stop.

"Why are you giving the third degree? Can't you see I'm having a very bad day. Please, back off."

"Okay," was all I said as we walked in.

She plopped down on the couch.

"So let's hear about your important meeting. How were you get away to a restaurant for such a long lunch?"

"No, it was...I mean we had a late break and I, I mean we...uuuh..."

Her response was interrupted by the doorbell. "Hold that thought," I said as I opened the door..

The police officer and I exchanged a few words before I walked him over to my wife. He looked down on her and asked,. "Are you Constance Keller?"

I could see her hands were shaking as she nodded in the affirmative.

"I'm detective O'Connors. I need to speak with you regarding your auto theft report. There appears to be a discrepancy regarding where the car was parked when it was stolen."

I played innocent and asked, "Connie, what's he talking about?"

Connie responded by puking all over the rug.

I ran to the bathroom and came back with a wastebasket and a roll of paper towels. Connie slumped into the chair while I cleaned up her mess. When I was finished I returned with a glass of cold water.

The detective didn't say a word. He simply intimidated the hell out of her by the way he stood lording over her as she sipped it. I stood next to him with my arms crossed.

"Mrs. Keller, do I have your permission to record this interview?"

"I guess so."

"Thank you. Let's start from the beginning. The restaurant has complimentary valet service but the car hiker is certain he didn't park your car. He's something of a gear head and said he would remember if your car was in his lot."

He began firing questions, "Who was your waitress? Where were you sitting? Do you have a charge card receipt? Were you with someone who could vouch for you? Mrs. Keller, can you explain how no one saw you or your very distinctive car?"

I could barely hear Connie's answer, "No sir."

He paused for dramatic effect then thumbed through his notes before resuming his interrogation, "You said after lunch you went shopping at the mall. "What stores did you shop at? What did you buy? Do you have any receipts?"

We live in a peaceful upper middle class suburb where not much happens on the night shift. The detective was playing this as though it was the return of Bonnie and Clyde.

Connie buried her face in her hands and began sobbing.

"Mrs. Keller you can answer now or we can go down to the station."

He was doing a beautiful job at building a trap.

"Mrs. Keller, would you like your husband to leave the room?"

She shook her head no.

"Mrs. Keller, I don't know if you were aware the Paradise Hotel videos every guest and their car as they arrive. I'll be picking up a copy of the surveillance tomorrow morning so if you want to amend your statement you should do it now."

I could see the life draining out of Connie's face. Gone was the cocky bitch who hung up on me at the hotel. I could barely hear her as she asked, "Do I need a lawyer?"

"You need to start telling the truth right now."

Silence.

"Do you realized I can place you under arrest for filing a false police report?"

"Jim, I'm so sorry. I only lied so you wouldn't get hurt." Then story of her affair spewed from her mouth.

Even though I knew how it ended the words tore through me. I was crying so hard I had to sit or my knees surely would have bucked.

When she finished she looked at me, her eyes pleading for mercy. Instead I turned away in disgust.

Detective O'Connors confirmed McAcree's phone number and place of employment-she didn't even know his home address-and said "I think I have everything I need."

"Are you going to arrest me?"

"I'll be meeting with the States Attorney in the morning. That'll be his call."

When he left Connie collapsed into a sobbing mass on the floor casting lamentations. "I'm so sorry I hurt you." Connie was flailing her arms to emphasize her words. "Jim, I love you. I never meant to hurt you."

"Do you hear what you're saying? You're not saying you're sorry you cheated...you're only sorry you got caught. Well guess what. You more than got caught...you got busted. I want to show you a video someone sent me today. I think you should sit down." I led her to the couch and helped her sit. I could feel her body trembling.

I hit the power button and our hi def TV sprung to life. Connie fainted dead out as she watched the video of her car pulling into the hotel parking lot.

While I waited for her to regain consciousness I opened my lap top and sent the same video to Mrs. Alan McAree. I followed this up with a phone call telling her to open the attachment if she wanted to know why her husband was late this evening. I could hear children in the background. "I'm very sorry but you need to watch this as soon as possible."

I stood over my soon to be ex-wife and waited. The video was running again when she regained consciousness. She looked catatonic; her eyes were hollow and bloodshot; tears poured down her face. What was left of her makeup made her look like a caricature of the beautiful woman I used to love. She stared in rapt horror as her betrayal played.

"I watched this video a dozen times hoping it would turn out to be a sick joke. I can't even begin to tell you how I feel when I watch you answer my phone call. I can hear you laughing as you hang up and kiss him again."

I couldn't make out what she was trying to say as she crawled over to me and collapsed at my feet sobbing. She reached out to touch me. I moved my legs out of her reach. "Don't touch me you filthy whore."

She began wailing like a banshee.

It didn't take much more than five minutes before Connie's cell phone rang. I grabbed it off the table; the ID said blocked caller. I answered with a whispered, "Alan," then put it on speaker.

The ruse worked; McAree thought I was Connie. "What the fuck is going on you fucking bitch!" He screamed. "My wife tore my head off for having an affair and threw me out. This is all your fault!" I hung up on him.

"What an asshole. You sure can pick 'em."

Connie's body began to convulse. She tried to talk but the sounds had forgotten how to become words.

"In case you think your day can't get any worse," I unlocked my attaché case, "I have something for you." On top of the stack of business papers was a document with Petition for Dissolution or Marriage in bold across the top.

I handed a copy to Connie. She started making strange gasping noises.

"I hope he was worth it. Now get out of my face. You disgust me."

Camilla (Forbidden)

Matt only has eyes for mom.

Camilla is the most beautiful woman I know. Most people wouldn't go that far. That's what love does. I don't know if love or the sexual desire came first, and it probably doesn't matter. I'm not talking about the usual love a son has for his mother. Very early on I knew that what I felt was different, and I never thought that I was wrong to feel it. Right from puberty I was very well adjusted to my maladjustment.

Camilla and I lived in New England without family and a smattering of friendly neighbors. Roy came and lived with us when I was seven, and left when I was sixteen. Roy filled in for my biological father who died when I was three. I wouldn't say we were close, but we stayed out of each other's way enough to make it a better relationship than some of my friends had with their 'Real' fathers. He usually came through when I needed him.

The thing I had for Camilla started as soon as I could feel what the word 'Sexy' meant. I think that concept starts in the eyes. Mom has sleepy eyes that seem to be an invitation; I guess that's why they call them bedroom eyes. It's more than fine when a woman has nice tits, great legs and all that. But that's not what makes someone sexy. It's how they carry themselves, and how they make you feel when they look at you.

It wasn't until I was older that I realized she had a killer body. Again, most people wouldn't go that far. It wasn't showy. In her clothes she looked more average than not. When I saw her in the bathroom getting dressed to go out one evening, I thought I had glimpsed perfection. To me she was a dime. She wasn't wearing a bra, but she was wearing panties, stockings, and heels. Oh my God.

Her breasts were a nice handful, long rather than round. Her nipples were large and capped the ends fully. Her legs were perfect, her ass was perfect, her skin was perfect. What can I say? I loved her by then, and then I loved her more.

I thought about her too much, if you consider all the time too much. Getting meshed with my mother filled my fantasies. I can't remember fantasizing about anyone else once I started on her. Watching her cooking, watching her walking, watching her watching TV, all fed the insatiable and inexhaustible scenarios I made up for us to engage in. No matter how bad a day I had, or how lonely I was, she would be waiting in my fantasy, dressed for sex, and saying something like, "It's okay baby, you'll feel better after you come in mommy's mouth." And I did feel better, even if it wasn't real.

It got so bad I started believing it myself. And when I would look at her I would think, 'How could she not know, how could she not feel what I feel, how could she not want what I want?' I was amazed at how normal our concerns and conversations were. And when we fought about the things mothers and sons fight over, and I was yelling at her, I knew that I was angry because I wasn't getting what I really wanted.

Mom was a bit of a neat freak and I'd heard the phrase, 'A place for everything and everything in its place,' one too many times, but it didn't really matter how many times she said that or, 'Matt, I need you to do this or that, Matt put this stuff away, Matt don't go out during the week, Matt be nice.' None of it mattered. The only thing that mattered was that Matt wanted his mother.

By the time I was eighteen, my friends and I had taken to drinking on the weekends. It escalated to a point where we got blasted beyond repair every Friday night. I hid it pretty well because mom didn't give me a hard time about coming home late on weekends, and I slept late enough the next day for it to wear off.

On the worst of these nights I walked into the house crunked in a stinking stupor. Mom was asleep on the couch with the TV on. I stood over her and looked while a current of electricity ramped up inside me. Her skirt was hiked up, displaying most of her creamy thighs. Her breasts were pressed together and some of her tit-flesh overflowed her bra. In reality, I wasn't seeing a hell of a lot, but it was enough to make me hear my own breath.

I wanted to reach in and take out her tit so I could suck on it. I wanted to take out my hardened cock and put it in her mouth. I wanted to push up her skirt and pull her panties down. And fuck her. I wanted. And there was a part of me that was telling me to take what I wanted. I walked away with the TV saying "Act now," because there was only one minute left to buy whatever they were selling.

After that night, I became wary of my own feelings, I started to think that maybe I was losing control of my fantasies. I wanted her so badly; I wasn't sure what I could do to make them come true. In that alcohol fed state all I could think of was taking her. The thought of hurting my mother or forcing her to do something she didn't want to, was enough to scare me. I didn't get drunk after that night, but I knew I had to get away.

The next day I said to mom, "I spoke to Roy and he said that I could stay with him; that's what I want to do."

She said, "Don't do that honey, just because we had a little fight, it doesn't mean anything, and he can't take care of you."

"I don't need him to," I said. "I only need a place to stay. One way or another I'm leaving mom, so you can be a pain about it, or just let me go."

She started to cry and said, "I can't do anything right; I can't even be a mother."

I felt like a shit, but I knew I had to leave. I said, "Mom, it's not because of the fight, or because of you. I just need to be alone for a while, away from this house. Look, I'll come over and see you; I'll only be across town. And anyway, I know how tight things are for you with them cutting back your time at work, and Roy said he'd pay for my stuff until I graduate." She cried. I wanted to hold her. I saw myself kissing her, caressing her, fucking her. I knew it was time to go.

Not living with Camilla made some things easier and some more difficult. I looked forward to seeing her and spending time with her, but I knew I couldn't be that close to her all the time. She didn't. She always hinted at how well we were getting along, and that I should think about moving back. I always equivocated.

I think I started growing up at Roy's because he gave me my independence, as long as I was responsible. I also grew up because of Bunny Spane. Bunny was a photographer that had an on and off thing going with Roy. She was probably a few years older than my mom, with tits too big to be real. She stayed over a lot and liked to talk all the time. Roy said it drove him crazy, but I liked that about her, because she would talk about anything and everything, and I learned a lot about women from talking to her. And since she was bi, I got different perspectives from our conversations. She even got me a few dates with some of the models. Nothing came of it but I definitely got comfortable around women, even if it was just to talk. The most serious I got was with a girl named Carol that I was with for five months who said I was never really 'There.' I guess it was true that I wasn't with her the way she wanted me to be, and so we broke up.

Mom came to my graduation and so did Roy. He even made a half-hearted play for her, but she didn't forget that he cheated on her. He told me about it while I stayed with him and said he'd made a mistake. I never confided in him or Bunny how I felt about mom. But about a month later, I confided in her.

I'd made a few bucks from the training program I was in, I was no longer a minor, and I felt a confidence I never had before. I was planning on finding a place of my own as soon as I could afford it. So I felt on top of it all when I went to my mother's for dinner. Maybe I wouldn't have said anything if she didn't look so hot. It wasn't as if she was walking around in lingerie or anything, but she had make-up on, and her legs looked so long in that pencil skirt, and her tits looked so touchable in that tighter than usual top.

We were having a beer with the casserole she'd made and I said, "Mom, you look so good."

She smiled and said, "Well, well."

I said. "I wish you weren't my mother." That ended her smile and a terrible painful look crossed her face that I thought would bring her to tears.

I said, "No mom, I didn't mean it like that, I'm glad you're my mother, but I wish we could be more than just a mother and son." She was baffled, and I could have stopped there with some lame remark about being friends or something, but I wanted her to know. I said "I love you mom." That cleared up nothing because I had rarely said it to her, maybe because I was afraid she'd hear it the way I meant it.

She looked at with an 'Are you okay?' look, and said, "Honey..."

I said, "Let me just tell you something. You're probably not going to like it, but I'm going to say it and then if you want me leave, I'll go. Mom I love you, and I've loved you for a long time...like a man loves a woman." She was at a loss. I said, "That's why I had to move out mom, I couldn't stand wanting you that way, looking at you, and not having you."

Finally she gathered herself. To her credit she didn't make believe she didn't know what I was talking about. She didn't say anything for a moment and I said, "Is that such a terrible thing mom?"

"No, Matt, it's not terrible...I guess other boys get a crush on their mothers sometimes, but you were young then, why wouldn't you be thinking about girls your own age?"

I said, "I was old enough; not that it matters...I don't know mom, ever since I can remember it's always been you...I want you."

She was obviously searching for something to say, and she gave a wan smile and said, "It's just a crush Mattie, you'll..."

"Mom, it's not a crush, I love you. And I see how unhappy you are, and I want to make you feel good, and I want to feel good with you. I know it's a crazy fantasy, but I think we could make each other happy. Mom, I'm as miserable as you are."

"Oh sweetheart, I'm sorry. I just don't know what to say, you tell me this, and I want to be here for you, but this is something I can't even get my mind around. I don't know what you want me to do."

To me it was obvious, but I wasn't ready to say the words, so I said, "I just want to be able to talk to you and tell you, and stop acting like things aren't the way they are for me. Just tell me if we can at least talk about this sometime, it doesn't have to be now."

She said, "Okay," but she was obviously still shell-shocked.

I said, "Thanks. Maybe I'll take off now. I'll call you." and I left.

I had gotten two blocks from her house when my cell rang and mom said, "Matt, I do want to talk to you; I don't want you to keep any of this from me. Would you please come back for a little while so we don't leave everything in a mess?"

I said, "Sure mom."

When I got back we sat together on the couch and mom said, "You said I was unhappy, and you're right. And one of the reasons is that you left, I missed you Mattie; at least now I understand some of why you went, but I don't want to lose you forever. So let's talk, but promise me you'll never do that again, go away without talking to me, no matter what it's about."

I said, "I just didn't know what to do then, I always wanted to tell you."

She said, "Okay baby, and promise me you'll give me time to absorb the shock from this bomb you just exploded in our living room."

I laughed, "Okay mom."

We talked for about two hours. Without being graphic, I told her I loved her and I wanted her. She listened and asked me about the when, what, and where, until she seemed to acclimate enough to the idea that I wasn't an alien that had taken over her son. She said, "The only inkling I had about any of this was the way you looked at me sometimes. I guess I felt it was sexual, but I thought it was...normal."

I sort of snickered, "To me it was normal; you looked hot."

She raised her eyebrows, shook her head side to side and said, "I don't know where you get that idea." We were both getting tired from the late hour and the emotional strain and I stood up and said, "I think I'll go now mom and we can talk again." When she stood I said, "But would you just do one thing for me, let me kiss you once, the way I've always wanted to?"

She said, "Alright baby." I leaned to her and she closed her eyes. I kissed her gently, not wanting to overdo it. Her mouth was slightly open and I slid my tongue between her lips only to the point where it touched the tip of her tongue." She made a small sound I wasn't sure of. I broke the kiss and said, "Thanks mom; was it terrible for you?"

She said, "Of course not baby, it was very...loving." I gave her a hug and enjoyed her body against me. I didn't let her feel my hard-on against her.

The next time we spoke on the phone, mom was worried about her job. She'd heard that some people were going to be cut and she didn't what she would do if it happened. I said, "I can help you out mom, I'm doing pretty good."

She said, "Oh no, thanks sweetheart, I'm okay for now." I really wanted to help out, but in reality, I didn't have that much extra cash. But I did get an idea. I spoke to Bunny Spane.

I called mom and said, "Invite me to dinner tonight."

She laughed, "Of course you're invited, you're always invited; you don't have to call, just come."

When I got there I said, "I know how you can make some decent money."

She said, "How?"

I said, "Pose."

She said, "What?"

I said "Listen, I know you don't think you're hot, but you are."

She said, "You my boy, are nuts." She laughed. "Pose for whom? Do I look like an eighteen year old Playboy Bunny?"

I said, "Mom I'm not kidding and I'm not nuts, but there is a Bunny involved. It's for an internet site of MILF's."

She said, "What's that?"

I said, "It doesn't matter, just listen. This is not hardcore or anything like that. It's more of a glamour thing. I know this woman Bunny who's a photographer for different internet magazines. One of them shows mature women in lingerie, stockings, corsets, stuff like that. I showed her a couple of pictures of you from the beach and she like them."

Mom said, "You showed her pictures? How do you know her?"

I didn't know if I should mention Roy but I figured it was best to be straight with her so I said, "I know her from Roy, and she's okay, a really nice person. Anyway, she said she'd take some pictures of you at her studio, and if she likes the way they come out, in a few months you could make enough to pay off everything you owe. And nothing goes on until you sign a release, so you can say no at any time."

Mom looked at me like I was crazy. "You think I'm going to pose nude and have it shown on some porn site?"

"Mom, I said it was just tease, not nude. And if it doesn't work out, or you decide not to do it after you meet Bunny, it's all off." It took me a while to convince her that she was good looking enough, and that she could do it, but the fact that she could be ahead of the money game for once finally turned the tide. I made an appointment for her.

I told mom that Bunny had outfits, or she could bring her own and she said, "I guess I'll pick something up."

When I asked if she wanted me to go with her, she said, "No silly."

I said, "I'd love to see in those outfits."

When she answered, "You'll see it when we go over there," my heart thumped because I didn't think she was going to let me watch her as she posed.

As we drove there, I said, "Mom, I didn't tell Bunny that I was your son, I just said you were a woman I know."

I wasn't sure how that would sit with her, but she said, "That's fine."

Bunny was her usual sweet, outrageous self when we arrived. We all had some wine and talked. Then she showed mom to the dressing room where she could change. When mom came out I was stoked. She had on black strappy heels and thigh high stockings that were vertically striped with alternate thin bands of black and grey sheer nylon. She had a black short slip on that ended above her stocking tops.

Bunny sized her up and said "Not bad, I love the shoes and stockings, but I'm not sure about that top. Wait a minute." She went into another room and came back with a black and white teddy. She said, "Try this Camilla, I think it'll work for you."

Mom went back into the dressing room and said, "I don't know Bunny, this may be too tight...and too much for me."

Bunny said, "Oh come on, let us just see it."

Mom came out and it was off the hook. The soft top of the teddy held mom's tits and made them look heavy. The material was tight enough so I could make out the outline of her big nipples. "Bunny said, "Oh, much better, now you look like a piece of ass." Mom laughed.

Bunny posed her in different moods to see what worked. She took a few shots of her looking sad, shy, dominant, and it wasn't until she made mom laugh, that things seemed to click for Bunny. She told her silly jokes like the one about the young polar bear at the North Pole that keeps asking his parents if he's a polar bear. When they want to know why he keeps asking, he says, "Because I'm fucking freezing." Mom laughed and had big grins on her face and Bunny kept shooting as she kept talking. When it was over, mom had a great time, and I had a hard-on.

Mom went into the dressing room and Bunny said to me, "Hey Matt, your girlfriend's got a great ass, and as I'm sure you know, definitely fuckable. If you ever give her up, tell her to give me a call." As we were leaving, I thought how when someone says something like that it can make you aware of something you know, but don't think about. I had never fixated on mom's ass, but I realized from her poses, she had an amazing well shaped butt. I knew it would find its way into a fantasy soon enough.

When we were in the car on the way home, I said, "Do you know what Bunny said to me?"

She said, "What," warily.

I said, "She said you had a great ass and were definitely fuckable."

She raised her eyebrows, covered her mouth and then laughed. I said seriously, "You do, and you are, mom."

She shook her head, smiled and said, "Boy you are naughty aren't you?" Naughty was much too mild for what I was picturing.

And talking about picturing, the next week, Bunny told me that they came out great, and she had sent a set to mom. Mom didn't offer to show them to me, but when I went over one night, I asked if I could see them. She reluctantly said okay. I said, "I'll bet I know where they are."

She said, "Where?"

I said, "In your underwear drawer." She laughed out loud and said, "How did you know?"

I said, "Mom, come on, you're so organized, that would be the best place to hide them and file them at the same time." Really I had taken a guess, but she got a big kick out of it.

When I saw them, she looked more like a model than a mom. I said, "Now tell me, do you look hot or not?"

She said, "Oh Bunny just made me look good." She looked better than good to me. Bunny had definitely captured the sweet vulnerability in mom's smile, and she definitely looked fuckable. I asked mom for a couple of the pictures and she said, "Okay, but if you show them to anybody, I'll kill you."

We talked for a bit and I was jazzed from looking at the photos and then I got kind of quiet when I thought I'd probably never see her taking things like that off for me. She said "What are you thinking about Mattie?"

I said, "When you were in school mom, did you ever have trouble going out with guys you liked?"

She thought for a minute and said, "I guess, not really."

I said, "It's different for a guy who likes someone he can't have."

She said, "But I know what it's like to not have the person you're looking for, the right person...I haven't been with a right person since your father died."

I said, "Well then I guess you do know how I feel." I just looked at her.

She said, "Oh Mattie, Mattie, what am I going to do with you?"

I said, "Well maybe you could just kiss me and then I'll take you home with me, at least on paper."

She kissed me, and again our tongues met. I put my hand on her boob and held it for a moment. It doesn't sound like a big deal to touch a woman's breast, but at that moment I was heart-poundingly elated. I had held my mother's tit and she didn't push my hand away. She did say with a capitulating smile, "Mattie you're so bad."

I said, "I'm not mom, I just love you." She put her head against mine and then I left. As far as the business with the pictures went, as it turned out, only a few days later, she called me and said, "Mattie I'm so excited, I got all my hours back at work. When I got called in I figured it was the end, but Jensen said that the people who stayed would pick up the slack and even get raises. Can you believe it?"

"Of course I believe it mom," I said. "You deserve it; you work harder than anyone over there."

She said, "Mattie, I called Bunny and told her I didn't want to put the pictures on the Net. You understand don't you?"

I said, "Sure mom, whatever you want."

She said, "I thought you might be disappointed because you seemed to like the idea so much."

"I just thought it would help you out financially, and of course I'm proud of the way you look, and it would have been a kick to see you up there, but it's cool. Anyway, I'd settle for a private showing, anytime."

She said, "Oh you..." But I do have a nice surprise. I had a nice talk with Bunny and when we were done she said that she had had two tickets for the Springsteen concert Friday night that she couldn't use. She asked if we'd like them. $250.00 seats Mattie, how's that?"

I said "Awesome mom."

She said, I'll tell you what, how about Tonio's for Pizza and Then the Parlour for sundaes after the concert?"

I said, "Deal."

Friday night was great. Bruce was sick; he just played and played. Our ears were buzzing from the concert and after sharing a banana split, mom said, "Mattie, It's been a long time since I had a good time like this...it was all wonderful."

After a moment she said, "I don't want the night to end; will you come home and stay a while, maybe sleep over?"

I said, "Sure," and I drove the long way, by the lake, and I said, "It's nice to see you feeling good mom." She smiled.

"Bunny said that you're a good guy, and I shouldn't hurt you." When she said it, I thought to myself, God that would be last thing I would ever do. I told her she had it wrong and she said, 'Come on Camilla, I see the way he looks at you, and the way you look at him.' I told her I'm thirty-six..."

I said, "Mom you're still thirty --five."

Mom said, "Anyway, we talked for about an hour and she told me how the girls she introduced you to, liked you, and wanted to keep going out, but you told them you loved someone else. She kept telling me that the real thing doesn't come around that often and you can't throw it away because some part of it isn't what it says in the manual. She said, 'Camilla, if someone doesn't think you fit together walking, well, fuck 'em.' I really like her Mattie. But then I started getting scared."

"About what mom?" I said.

She took a deep breath and said, "The other night when you touched me, it didn't feel wrong. And I kept thinking about what Bunny said, and I thought it's been eighteen years since I've been loved the way I need to be, and how many chances do you get in life?"

At this point we'd reached the house and I didn't say anything because my head was starting to swirl. When we got inside mom kept talking and said, "Mattie, I was also scared when you touched me because I thought how easy it would be to let myself love you, because it was what I was feeling anyway. And what seemed impossible to me just a little while ago doesn't anymore."

She took a deep breath and blew it out slowly. Then she said, "Mattie...I'm saying yes. I'm saying yes to really loving you and letting you love me. God I hope it doesn't turn into a disaster, but I guess anything could...so, even though I'm scared out of my mind, I'm saying yes."

I was almost knocked out cold. Instead of saying some loving thing, I had to make sure of what I was hearing, so I said, "Mom, I just couldn't take it if this is some kind of game, or a way to get me to come home, or if you're teasing me. Mom, are we going to have sex?"

She said, "Yes darling, we're going to have sex."

I said, "Now?"

She laughed, "Now."

I unbuttoned her shirt slowly as if I were expecting her to stop the whole thing and say, "Just kidding." She didn't. Nor did she do anything to help me undress her. I reached back and after a few seconds, I unhooked her bra.

When her tits were exposed, I could see the fullness that didn't show in her clothes. They looked swollen, as if she were having her period or pregnant, especially since her nipples were so large and pronounced. I held her bare tit in my hand and was almost mesmerized by it. I must have been looking and holding it for a long time when mom smiled and said, "Aren't you even going to kiss me when you do that?"

I sort of woke up and said, "Oh yes mom, I'm going to kiss you, and everything else." We kissed and her mouth and tongue told me that she wasn't going to stop me. Each kiss was different and took me to unexpected places. Still in disbelief I undid her skirt and said, "I love you mom."

She said, "I know baby, and I know that's why you want to have sex with me - God, I hope that's why you want to have sex with me, because that's how I feel baby, I want you because I love you."

I said, "Yes mom, of course it's because I love, because I've always loved you. You have to know that mom."

She said, "Yes baby, I know it. Tell me what you want."

I urged her towards the bed and she sat. I said, "I want to look at you mom." She raised herself slightly and I took my mother's panties off. She wasn't wearing stockings, and the creamy, even tone extended from where her feet touched the floor up to her pussy. I put my hands on her knees as she opened her legs without much prompting. I leaned over and kissed the inside of her thigh and then kissed the exhilarating sight before me.

She said, "OH," and twitched in surprise since I had placed my lips directly on her clit. Carol was the first girl I had kissed there and she had shown me exactly where and how to do it. I was grateful to her as I heard my mother's sounds when I began sucking and tonguing the swelling button. She said, "Oh baby, easy, or you'll make me come too fast."

I eased up and teased her clit more than working it. The honey coming from my mother's pussy was the sweetest thing this young son had ever tasted. I was amped and mom was ready. Even as I held my cock and brought it to her opening, I couldn't believe it was going to happen. Her folds split to allow me entry and her pussy held me in a firm grasp as I pushed my way in. The walls of her passageway were like velour. I pushed in and out slowly, fighting the urge to piston my way to a quick orgasm. Mom said, "Ohh, Mattie, you're inside me, Ohh, God, Ohh, Ohh, sweetheart..." She said, "Ohh," each time I gave her the full length of my cock.

I said, "Mom, I waited so long to do this and it feels even better than I thought it would. I love you mom."

She said, "Yes Mattie, yes, yes, I'm glad, I'm so glad you're inside me, Oh God..."

If I could live in one moment forever, that would be it. Spreading open my mother's pussy with the full width and length of my cock as she moaned, feeling her velvety pussy massage my shaft as we moved together, melting into one another.

After a few minutes of floating in the exquisite sensations, I gazed at the place where we were connected and said, "Mom, look at how beautiful we are together."

She opened her eyes and saw what I was seeing. She said, "Yes baby it is beautiful and you're beautiful. Ohh honey it feels so good. I didn't imagine it would feel so good having you inside me." She closed her eyes again and said, "Ohh darling, Ohh darling, Ohh darling..." as I changed the angle and pushed one of her legs out wider. My mother was so opened for me, the sight of her splayed legs almost made me come.

As I fucked her I said, "Mom, I tried to find someone who could take your place, but I never did. It was you I wanted, only you."

She said, "Yes baby, I'm glad. I'm here now; I'm yours. You don't have to look anymore. Momma's here whenever you want her. OH...Ohhhh...yes, like that sweetheart, like that."

My cock was a steel pipe as it entered and left her pussy. I pushed in as far as I could go and stayed there, up against her ass. Mom let out a long, "OHHhhh..." as I moved my hips and the rod that was inside her. When I started pumping again she said, "Oh Mattie, I'm going to come, OH, OH, OHHHhh..." She arched her back and I went into her deeper and harder than I had before and I heard her yell "AAiiiiii...MAAATIEEE..." Her cry of pleasure filled the room.

I was so happy to hear her coming, I said, "Yes mom come, come..." My mother was coming for me, on me, and I pumped hard to join her. After five or six more strokes into her pussy I crossed the threshold and began pouring my cum into my mother's opening.

I was almost as loud as she was as I let go of the cords of sperm I had been saving for her. Even as I came I felt it was a wonder that I was shooting my seed into my mother's womb. My orgasm was long and satisfying and we were both drenched as I finished and stayed inside her. She held me tight and kissed me.

I said, "Are you sorry mom?"

She said, "No baby, I'm happy, it was wonderful and I haven't been happy to be with someone like this for a long time."

I said, "Well there's no question about it now, Bunny was right, you are definitely fuckable."

She laughed and said, "OH you...," and gave me a poke, and then a kiss. Then she said in my ear, "And so are you baby. I had forgotten what great sex was like. My darling son...I can't believe how good we are together."

I said, "Because we were made for each other. This was made for me." I covered her wet pussy with my palm. "And this was made for you." I put her hand over the shaft that was glazed with our juices.

She said, "Yes baby, it is," and she went to take it in her mouth. She sucked the head a few times and then licked around, and down. It didn't take long for my cock to become fully erect again. Mom said, "Bunny told me that there was nothing like strong young cock at our age, one that can keep going; she was right." She grabbed my stiff shaft and said, "This belongs to Camilla now; God, you filled me up so good with it baby."

I said, "Yes mom, and I'm going to fill you with it all the time now; I'm not going to stop.

She said, "Mmm," in assent as she closed her lips around the swollen head. Mom moved up and down on me, sucking hard whenever she came back to the tip. She surprised me with how quickly she amped me up with her mouth and hands working together. I guess I shouldn't have been surprised; it was the woman I had been fantasizing about for years, and I was in her mouth. My mother was sucking me.

She continued working my shaft and making sounds that told me she was taking pleasure in what she was doing to me. She opened her mouth for a moment to say, "Yes, my baby, my baby."

She held my sack and her warm hands made me want to explode in her mouth. She rubbed and massaged my balls as she sucked. I said, "Yes mom, yes, don't stop sucking me, yes, suck your boy, suck me, suck me, suck me..." I kept saying it as the most intense feeling reached the point of eruption, and when I couldn't stand it anymore, I cried out "MOM..." and let it go. I detonated a volley of cum into my mother's mouth. Once I started, I couldn't stop coming. I came more than I did in her pussy and still she tightened her lips around my cock and drew more of my juice into her mouth with each suck in. I could only repeat, "OH, OH, OH..." as each discharge shook me. When I was finally done, I realized that she had swallowed it all.

She said, "Baby, I love you so much and I'm going to make you happy, I'm going to make us happy." I had finished coming, but mom seemed to get even more excited; she was breathing hard and saying. "Now you have a momma who takes care of you the way you need, don't you baby?" I did. I had a mother who loved me enough to let me come in her mouth.

I said, "Yes mom, that's how I need to be loved, and that's how I need to love you."

She sucked me more, taking a lot of my hardening cock into her mouth. She said "Mmmm, yes baby, love me more baby, come some more in mommy's mouth, come in mommy's mouth, mmmm..." I didn't think I could get hard and stoked so fast, but I did. While she was sucking, she was alternately rubbing my balls and stroking on my shaft. In only a minute or two, I was thinking about coming again. She didn't let up. I was trying to slow her down, but she was having none of it. She squeezed the base of my cock and ran her finger over my balls. Between her hands and mouth there was too much stimulation.

I started saying, "Mom, mom," to stop her, but her insistent sucking pushed me over the edge. I held her head and said, "Mom I'm coming again." It almost came out as a scream as the first exquisite release shot into her mouth.

She kept going and made an "Mmm..." sound that had a joyful quality to it. I poured more cream into her mouth and down her throat until I was exhausted and depleted. When she finally stopped sucking, I was in a heap. As I started to recover I said,

"Mom, if that's an example of what it's going to be like being together, you're going to have a very happy son."

"And you're going to have a very happy mom," she said, "As soon as you're inside me again."

Well, it's been going on more than a year now, and we've both been right.

CPSIA information can be obtained
at www.ICGtesting.com
Printed in the USA
LVHW021023291220
675197LV00001B/80